GM01158424

The Colour (

An intriguing mix of fact and folklore from a master storyteller, '**The Colour of Life**' is set mainly around Waterford and Woodstown in the 1930s.

Geoff Cronin gives us a rich insight into a time that has almost been forgotten. He reveals the joy of an almost idyllic childhood and brings to life, in his own inimitable style, the fascinating characters who inhabited his world.

His sharp and witty observations are hauntingly evocative of a bygone age, giving a unique and vivid view of a way of life that has now vanished.

At times downright funny, this is a charming, well told, series of cameos that will appeal to all ages.

The Colour
of Life

Geoff Cronin

Moyhill Publishing

First Published in 2005 by Moyhill Publishing

A CIP catalogue record for this book is available from the British Library.

ISBN 1-905597-00-2
ISBN 978-1-905597-00-0

Designed & typeset by *Moyhill* Publishing
Cover Photograph by author

Printed in UK

Book Sales in Ireland and UK
Moyhill Publishing,
12 Eaton Brae, Shankill, Co. Dublin, Ireland.

Book Sales in continental Europe
Moyhill Publishing,
Avenida Sicilia 54, 28420 Galapagar, Madrid, Spain.

Order online at *http://www.moyhill.com*
or **e-mail** *orders@moyhill.com*

Dedication

This book is dedicated to my family, without whose
constant encouragement it might never have been written.

Acknowledgements

The ship photographs which appear in "My Grandfather's Story" are from paintings by Pierse Murphy. These paintings were donated to the Waterford Municipal Art Collection by Gerald Spencer and family.

Contents

Introduction.. iii

1. Pigeons.. 1

2. My Grandfather's Story 7

3. The Crane... 19

4. The Miser... 23

5. The Rules (Woodstown) Of Pitch And Toss
   And How To Play It....................................... 26

6. Woodstown In The 1930s.................................. 29

7. Woodstown Cricket Club 32

8. The Art Of Making Snares 35

9. How the Stable Was Built................................ 40

10. The Devil Finds Work...... ,,,,,,,,,,,,,,.............. 46

11. The Financier and The Farmer's Wife 59

12. The Hound From Hell.................................... 64

13. The Station... 68

14. The Price Of A Habit 73

15. The Gun... 76

16. The Shop.. 82

17. James the Landlord...................................... 97

18. The Snipe Shoot... 105

19. Work on a Timber Gang 109

20. The Digs In Dublin...................................... 119

21. The Nuns At The Glue Pot.............................. 130

22. The Mobile Cinema 134

23. The Ferguson Tractor 138

24. Whiskey And Its Disciples.............................. 147

i

Contents

25. The Dance Scene 150

26. Retention 162

27. The Haul Of Bass 164

28. The Rosary 169

29. Tommy And The Fish 172

30. The Power Of Prayer 174

31. The Tangler's Hat 177

32. The Turkey Run 182

33. Salad And Omelets In Kritsa 187

34. Sangria 192

Note: The dates shown under individual chapter titles relate to either the year of the event or the year in which I first wrote the story.

Introduction

I was born at tea time at number 12 John Street, Waterford on September 23rd 1923. My father was Richard Cronin and my mother was Claire Spencer of John Street Waterford. They were married in St John's Church in 1919.

Things are moving so fast in this day and age – and people are so absorbed, and necessarily so, with here and now that things of the past tend to get buried deeper and deeper. Also, people's memories seem to be shorter now and they cannot remember the little things – day to day pictures which make up the larger canvas of life.

It seems to me that soon there may be little or no detailed knowledge of what life was *really* like in the 1930s in a town – sorry, I should have said City, in accordance with its ancient charter – like Waterford. So I shall attempt to provide some of these little cameos as much for the fun of telling as for the benefit of posterity.

Geoffrey Cronin
29 July 2005

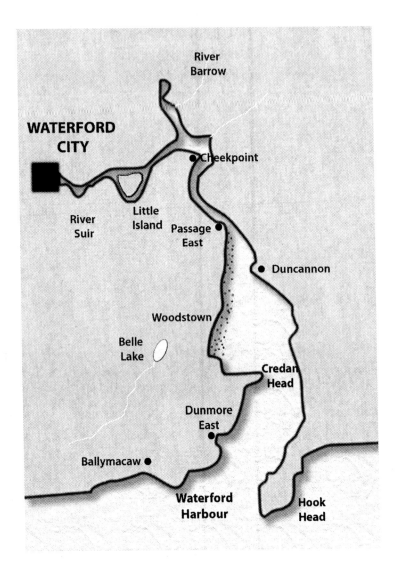

Pigeons

1929

In my early childhood, my family and I lived over our Bakery Shop at number 12 John Street, Waterford, which my father owned. Being the beginning of the city's main street, it was a busy place, and one of the features of it was the Apple Market. This took place in a large open area, bordered by small shops, where the apple farmers who were mostly from the Kilkenny side of the river Suir, assembled every Saturday morning.

Their horses would be tethered around the Fountain Clock, at the north end of the area, and their carts, full of apples, would be "shafts down" along the edge of the street and around in a long oval shape to face the shops on the far side. The carts would be divided internally into boxes where the apples would be displayed – Honeyballs, Pippins, Woodcocks and Ladies Fingers for eating, and cookers like Bramleys, hard, green and sour, all shining in their nests of clean hay and presenting a truly Technicolor picture of a market place.

Local children, including myself, delighted with this cornucopia of deliciousness would wander in and out between the carts "admiring" the displays and buying the odd pennyworth of those deep red Honeyballs which oozed the nectar of red ripeness – they sold for ten a penny – and many a feast would ensue as groups of us gathered in the archway which led off the market and into Hartrey's sweet factory.

The conversations on these occasions were not at all like those that children of today would have, for many of these children would be in bare feet, as indeed were some of their parents, and they lived in the lanes and tenements which surrounded the area at that time. At age six, I knew all these places and I played and chatted with kids from The Model Lane, The Back Lane, Newports Lane, Spring Garden Alley, Little Mickle Street, The Tanyard Arch, and New Street Tenements, which were four-storey Georgian houses, where families of six to ten people lived in each room, with no running water and no electricity and one outside toilet. On the stairways there were neither banisters nor handrails because the tenants would have used these as firewood. There was no class distinction among the kids, who were "just kids" after all.

Topics of conversation at the apple feasts would be about cage birds, finches and linnets, dogs, ferrets and the favourite was *Pigeons*. There were thirteen corn stores in the city at that time, and the men employed there had access to the screenings and sweepings of the store and this meant they could keep a few pairs of pigeons for very little money, and the children learned all about pigeons quite naturally.

In addition, there was a magazine "Pigeons and Pigeon World" price threepence, which came in from England and had about forty pages of nothing else but pigeons – Homers, Tumblers, Tipplers, Rollers, Nuns, Turbits, Fantails, Pouters, Booted, Bare Legs, and of course the Feral Pigeons, called locally "Rogs", which were good for nothing but scavenging.

The more I learned the more fascinated I became with the whole pigeon scene – and the descriptions of how the

birds were coloured enthralled me. I very quickly learned the jargon, and could describe any bird I saw. There were Blue Barred, Blue Check, Red Mottled, Black Badged, Blue Baldhead, Snow White, Jet Black, Red Check and top of my list, the one that really fired my imagination, was Silver Dun.

By the time I was eight, I had acquired many a Rog, because that was all the local kids had to sell for three or four pennies. Mind you, I never managed to get a Silver Dun, but by then I knew that the colour of a bird did not make him truly bred to a particular breed. I had watched every pigeon I could see, and I knew a racer from a tumbler or a roller, but then other things were happening in my life at this point.

My family was moving to live in Woodstown, a seaside location eight miles from the city, and while it was quite a

change from John Street and the apple market, the freedom of actually living on a beach was truly wonderful. A further bonus was that I now had a shed in which I could keep pigeons properly.

I wasted no time in acquiring a pair of Blue Barred racing (Homing) pigeons, which I installed in my shed. It was ill appointed

4

for the purpose of accommodating a pair of breeding birds, and I was flat broke having spent my entire savings buying them.

When I noticed the hen collecting straws and carrying them to a corner of the floor I realized that she was nesting. I ran to tell my mother the news, and to ask her to advance me five shillings to buy a nest box I saw advertised in my pigeon magazine.

"No," she said, "Make one yourself, there's wood and tools in the garage."

"But Mother," I said, "I don't know how."

"Come on boy," she answered. "I'll show you how" and she did just that.

The measurements were taken from the magazine, and the wood marked out, and then I was left to get on with it. The job was slow and painful, and I had two black and bruised fingernails at the end – my aim with the hammer was unpractised – but after a day and a half I had succeeded and I took my handiwork to show my mother.

"Well done," she said, "now paint it," and before I could protest, she took my arm and said "Come on boy, I'll show you," and she did.

When the paint had dried, I took the box to show her, and after examining it she said "Very well done boy, it's just as good as the one in the magazine and you must see if the hen will take to it."

I turned to take it to the shed when she called me back and put five shillings into my hand saying "That's what you earned by doing the job yourself. Never forget that anything you can do with your two hands is money."

Claire Spencer-Cronin
Circa 1918

Well, the hen took to the box and nested in it and in eighteen days her two downy chicks arrived and grew into fine strong birds, and thus began a life-long passion for all kinds of pigeons.

And I never forgot the lesson my mother taught me.

If something was scarce and difficult to come by
it was described as being
"*as plentiful as feathers on a frog!*"

My Grandfather's Story

1930

Geoffrey Spencer, my maternal grandfather, born of a farming family in County Waterford about 1830, was not the eldest son of that family, and as such, he could not expect to inherit the family farm, and instead he would be "fortuned off". He would be given a cash inheritance, the size of it being determined by the amount of money available at the time, and after due consideration was given to the rights of other family members. Since most of a farmer's cash would be locked up in livestock, land and crops, actual cash would not be plentiful at the best of times. However, family history has it that in or about

Geoffrey Spencer

1850 Geoffrey Spencer came into Waterford City with £100 in his pocket to seek his fortune in some area other than farming.

When he walked down the quay, and bear in mind that ships of all shapes and sizes would have been tied up three abreast for some miles up river waiting to unload, he came upon a group of merchants having a heated debate about a particular ship which was for auction that day. The point at issue was that the ship, a 200 ton Barquentine, was moored in the river and it was rumoured that her bottom was not sound and she was to be sold "as she stood", as nobody was prepared to pay the cost of pulling her up on the graving bank to examine the bottom, least of all the owner. This fact served to strengthen the rumour that "she had worm in the bottom".

A Barquentine has three or more masts with square sails only on the foremast. The "Madcap" is shown above.

In any event, the auctioneer arrived on the scene and set the auction in train, and the young Spencer, knowing nothing whatsoever about ships and sensing the possibility of a bargain, bid £100 for the ship. There was no other bid and she was knocked down to him.

Now there was such interest and controversy about the ship that a group of merchants offered to have her pulled up on the graving bank and examined, and they would share the cost. Geoffrey Spencer offered no objection to this, as it was very much in his interest to know if he had a sound ship, and she was duly hauled up. After minute examination by the port surveyor, she was pronounced sound. The gamble had paid off!

One man who had shown a keen interest in the proceedings was a Mr. Nelson, a local bank manager, who congratulated my Grandfather on his purchase, and told him the ship was worth at least £400, and that he could use her as collateral to finance a voyage cross-channel. I must assume that he gave my Grandfather advice on how best to make use of the ship, because he subsequently engaged a Captain Cummins as skipper, a crew was hired and she sailed off to Wales with the young Spencer on board to bring back a cargo of coal. The cargo he sold piecemeal on the side of the quay and thus began his career as a coal merchant and ship owner.

In the course of his travels to the Welsh coalfields, my Grandfather learned how the mine operated, and he realized that there were many mines and they all needed two things to function. They needed pit props to support the mineshafts, and also ponies to draw coal from the face to the loading points. These were the early days of mining and the needs were basic.

Armed with this information, he set up a trading arrangement with the Welsh mines, and I only know the name of one of them – it was the Powell Duffryn Coal Company (Originally started by Thomas Powell around 1837). He would bring over a cargo of pit props and ponies, and bring back a cargo of coal.

This worked out very well, as he knew all about horseflesh from the farming, and also there was an abundance of suitable timbers to be had, so he was soon showing handsome profits, there being a strong market for coal at the Waterford end.

From "The Penny Magazine"

Over time the balance or trade swung so much in his favour that he was able to acquire shares in several mines, which subsequently would prove to be very valuable indeed.

As the Spencer business grew, he purchased a berth in Waterford Harbour, just above the bridge on the Waterford side of the river. He engaged the services of a Captain Furness to skipper a second ship, called (I believe) The Zada. His first ship was the Madcap, and he had at least four other ships, but I don't know all their names. They were mainly

Barquentine sailing ships of about 200 tons. This was the common size of coasters of the period, and they would have been two or three-masted schooners.

There are paintings of some of his ships in one of Waterford's Museums – in the Waterford Municipal Art Collection.

Geoffrey Spencer was married twice. His first wife was Johanna Lyons, and his second wife was Minnie O'Keefe from Lisnakill, Co. Waterford. Only two sons from his first marriage survived to adulthood, and they were David and Jim.

David worked in the coal business with his father, and died in his thirties. Jim worked a farm in Kilcohan, which his father had acquired. He later set up a dairy business in Johnstown, Waterford, which was still going in the 1960s, run by his family.

The "Oriental"

My grandfather was a born entrepreneur. He lived on the corner of John Street and Waterside, and his premises consisted of a large coal yard, big enough to hold two or three cargos of coal, and a pub with living quarters, where he raised two families. His second family by Minnie O'Keefe consisted of Joe, the eldest, Frank and a daughter, Claire, who was my mother.

His second wife died when my mother was three years old, and she recalled, even in her old age, the horror of being lifted up to kiss her dead mother good-bye, as she lay in her coffin.

At age four my mother went into the Ursuline Convent as a boarder, and because her father was "in trade", the nuns were reluctant to accept her. However, I guess that, because of his considerable wealth at that stage, he probably made them an offer they could not refuse. I believe that the Ursuline nuns, at that time, were recruited from families who held titles and such like. At any rate, they were regarded very much as "top drawer". My mother was a boarder there until she left school.

To get back to Spencer the entrepreneur, he built a row of houses, including "the dairy" in Johnstown, as an investment. He owned a limekiln, and a large piece of land in Poleberry, which his son David sold (while drunk) to a local builder who shall be nameless.

I should tell you that in those days, owning a limekiln was equivalent to owning a cement factory today. More building was done then using lime mortar than cement, which was still a novelty. Part of the business of a lime-works then was the supply of fresh-water sand, and the source of this was an inexhaustible series of sand banks in the river Suir, about ten miles up-river at Fiddown. "Lighter men", who owned dumb barges – they had no engines – would pole their way up-river on the flood tide and anchor at the sand bank of their choice.

They lived on the barge, or lighter, as they were some-times called, and during the hours of daylight, they would single-handedly shovel sand into the hold of the barge until she was full – I think they held up to sixty or seventy tons – which took almost two weeks. They then cast off on full tide, and poled the barge down river in stages whenever the water was slack. When they got to the Scotch Quay, they poled their way up the tributary, through the park, and moored at John's Bridge on the Waterside, and there they would unload on the quayside, which meant a week or ten days shovelling again. Incidentally there was a limekiln just at this point. The river was, however, navigable for lighters up to where the Spencer limekiln was situated. This was a strategic advantage for that kiln, as limestone – the raw material – as well as fresh-water sand could be delivered onto the actual site of the lime works.

The same river, being tidal, powered a grist mill situ-ated just above John's Bridge. There was a tunnel running under that mill, which had a sluice gate on it. The gate was open while the tide was coming in, allowing the water to flow through to the Millers Marsh, and thence up the water lane, which went up the back of St. Ursula's Terrace, and

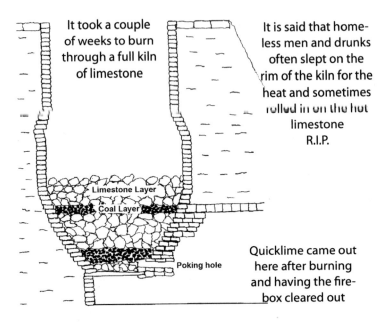

It took a couple of weeks to burn through a full kiln of limestone

It is said that homeless men and drunks often slept on the rim of the kiln for the heat and sometimes rolled in on the hot limestone
R.I.P.

Limestone Layer

Coal Layer

Poking hole

Quicklime came out here after burning and having the firebox cleared out

The quicklime could be "slaked" by pouring water on it, turning it into hydrated lime powder and used for making whitewash or mortar or dressing land for certain crops.

Pathway to top of kiln for loading

Typical Lime Kiln of the 18/1900s

formed the headrace for the mill. The sluice gate was closed at full tide, locking in the full of the headrace, and as the tide receded, the gate was opened and the outflow of water drove the mill wheel, which was undershot.

Geoffrey Spencer lived at the pub/coal-yard until his death in 1917 at the age of 80 years. He went to seven o'clock Mass every day of his life, and *never* wore an overcoat. When he died, apart from his property, he left £60,000 in cash, his shares in the Welsh mines, a full yard of coal and a concrete barge full of coal on the berth at the quay, and his ships. He was the last man in Waterford to own a fleet of sailing ships. His total estate, with the exception of £1,000 and the family silver left to my mother, was left to his son Joe.

A farm of approx. 100 acres at Ballindud, Co. Waterford, which my grandfather had inherited from his brother-in-law John Lyons, went to the youngest son Frank, and is still in Spencer ownership. The smaller farm at Kilcohan, was assigned to Jim Spencer, the only survivor of the first marriage, and up to recently, was in Spencer ownership, when it was sold for some millions to a supermarket chain.

Here ends my knowledge of Geoffrey Spencer, a man of great business acumen, who made his mark on Waterford of the Ships in no uncertain way. He is buried in Ballygunner Cemetery, and over his grave stands probably the most impressive monument there – a white marble figure of Christ carrying his cross. R.I.P.

The inscription reads

ERECTED
IN GRATEFUL AND AFFECTIONATE
REMEMBRANCE
OF
OUR DEAR FATHER
BY THE LOVING CHILDREN OF

Geoffrey Spencer

WATERFORD
WHO DIED 9TH APRIL 1917 IN HIS 80TH YEAR

Unique Historic Pictures Recently Discovered
No. 7 – A Quayside Scene

THIS is, indeed, a perfect specimen of a quayside scene in Waterford, sixty years ago. On the extreme right is seen the old "nopper" dredger of the Waterford Harbour Commissioners, with its twenty-four buckets. Mr. J. Kehoe was the dredging master, and it was then an important operation, for the mud was regarded as a very valuable fertiliser for the farmers. The "Lighters," a type of oar-propelled barge rather peculiar to the port, certainly not in common use, took loads of the mud from the dredger. Then the "lighters" set forth on the tide, as a rule, for tributaries of the river Suir, such as the Kilmacow Pill, and delivered the mud to farmers, who carted it to their lands. It is said that because of the facility provided by the Kilmacow Pill in transporting this chemically rich river mud, the district of Kilmacow is so very fertile. Of course, it is also a limestone locality, but the two combined have made this district one of the richest in Ireland in agricultural produce.

Note:
Although the article states that the lighters were "*oar*-propelled", they were actually "*pole*-propelled".

The barquentine seen prominently is the "Madcap," which was owned by the late Mr. Geoffrey Spencer, Coal Merchant, Waterford, who imported coal direct from the Welsh coalfields. He was father of Mr. J. V. A. Spencer, St. Bernard's, Tramore, the well-known tomato-grower, and grandfather of Mr. Gerald Spencer, Ashgrove, Moonmin, Co. Kilkenny. The master of this imposing vessel was the late Captain Nicholas Cummins, Ballybricken, whose children are well-known and esteemed Waterford citizens to-day. Afterwards, Mr. Spencer purchased the "Zayda" and appointed Capt. Cummins master of that new addition, the late Capt. Furniss, The Glen, Waterford being appointed master of the "Madcap."

The vessel seen in the right background is a barque, one of the largest of all sailing vessels, which was probably carrying a cargo of grain from Australia or South America. They used anchor in mid-river whilst awaiting a place at Hall's wharf, further up the river. In the barkground (left) can be seen the creosote factory, where railway sleepers were dressed. This was afterwards replaced by the box factory, which is, now, of course, no longer in existence. In the distance is the spire of the Chapel-of-Ease. When they demolished the old chapel, which was much smaller than the present Church of the Sacred Heart, the builders left the spire standing. Whilst the present beautiful church was being erected, Holy Mass and other divine services were held in a building on the East side of Sion Row.

Newspaper clipping from
"The Munster Express" – July 11th 1952

18

The Crane

1930

The Grey Heron was always known as "the Crane" among the locals of Woodstown when I was growing up there. A large and apparently solitary bird, frequenting bog holes and other lonely places, it fascinated those of us who hunted rats, and anything that moved, along the banks of the streams near our home.

For my own part, I found the mysteries of nature so amazing that I was able to believe most of the lore I was able to glean by talking to those more knowledgeable than myself in that pursuit. Often I stood quietly and listened avidly to the conversation of the local men when they sat on the stone at the "Gap" of a summer's evening, smoking their blue fumed pipes, or playing a hand of cards on the balding grass patch where the sand showed through.

It was in this way I learned all about the crane; how he had only one long gut and was so nervous that if you could get near him and make a really loud noise, he would drop dead – "and why wouldn't he, with only one gut. Sure it stood to reason."

Another well proven fact was that if a man were to shoot a crane, on purpose, or even by accident, that man would never be able to father a child. Indeed I heard that precise reason given as to why a neighbour and his wife had no family. The fact that they were both in their fifties when they wedded seemed not to enter into the particular discussion

It was on one of my listening sessions that I heard the following story, declared at the time to be "as true as Jazes." Here it is as near verbatim as my pen will reach:-

⚜

"Meself and another fella were down in the lower village of Cheekpoint one evening near sunset and we were sitting on the wall by the bank of the river watchin' the shallows to see if there was any fishin'. T'was a weak tide, slow and still by the bank where the water was slack and you could see the mudbank beginning to show up the river a piece. We were there thinking of nothing at all when down floated an auld crane, and dropped into the shadow of the bank in a few inches of water. We were looking down on him from above and could see him as clear as anything.

They're very nervous, ye know, and of course they have only one gut inside in 'em.

Anyway, he stood there, still as a stone, takin' in everythin' We never moved and after a while he began to stroll around slowly, watchin' the water to see would he find his supper – they ate crabs and small fishes and that class of thing.

Did you ever see the way he walks? Well, I'll tell ye; he never lifts the foot out of the water and never a ripple even though his feet are as long as your hand. Lookin' at him goin' along like that, you'd think he couldn't move fast, but upon me song, you'd be wrong! Wait till I tell ye now – the next thing we saw was yer man (the crane), frozen still, like a stick lookin' down be the side of a rock and his neck crooked back like an "S-hook", and not a stir out of him.

I thought bejazes he was gone asleep, when quick as a flash down went his head into the water – and you know they have a bake like a feckin' harpoon – up came the head again and he had a fair sized eel caught in his bake.

Well, straight away, he lifted his head up in the air, opened the bake, and down the gullet went the eel – it was all over in a second – but hauld on now till you hear...

Off he went, strollin' like before, but he wasn't gone three yards when out came the eel wriggling out of the crane's arse and dropped into the water – they have only one gut ye see, and there was nothin' to stop the eel goin' right through yer man.

Well if that crane moved fast when he first caught that eel bejazus he moved twice as fast now. Round he swung, took a step a yard long, down went the bake and up again like a flash with that eel caught again. He paused for a second and swallowed the eel for the second time.

We thought that was that, and the oul' crane had bested the eel, but true as God, we were wrong again. No sooner did the crane start to walk again, than out of his arse wriggled that eel again, and down into the water he dropped. By this time, we were looking out of our mouths at the carry on. We never seen the like before.

Well, bejazus boy, lighnin' was slow compared to the speed at which that crane turned and dived on the eel for the third time, and he caught him tight in that big bake. He wasn't goin' to be done out of his supper, d'ye see. But now, he didn't swallow the eel this time. Instead, he held him in his bake and commenced to look around slowly. After a while he walked in to where there was a fair sized rock stickin' up-out of the water. An' then bejazes, didn't he turn his back to the rock, lifted his tail, sat down on the rock, and swallowed the eel with one gulp. Well he sat there for a full ten minutes until, I suppose, the eel smothered inside him. At any rate, when he walked off through the water, that eel never appeared again. And that's a fact boy – there's cranes for you now!!"

The Miser

1931

When I was a boy, in the early 1930s, there was always music in our house. My mother was an accomplished pianist and singer and my father had a very fine tenor voice. He would sing songs such as *The Trumpeter, Songs of Araby, The Toreador's Song* from Carmen and *Friend of Mine* and my mother would play the accompaniment on the piano. They sang many duets also and on wet days and Sundays as children we would gather round the piano and mother would play all the popular and comic songs of the day. A right old sing-song would be enjoyed by all. I vividly remember my favourite, which was *"Minnie the Moocher"*!

Both my parents were heavily involved in the Wallace Grand Opera Society in its heyday and consequently they knew everybody in the musical scene of the day and most of their friends came from that circle.

Two of their friends who often visited us were a Jewish couple, Isaac Levi and his wife Florence, whose maiden name was Goldring. They were immigrants from Poland and had fled from there in the early 1900s when Jews were being persecuted. Incidentally, they told me that they had been promised in marriage to each other when they were children. Classical music was their forte and they often regaled us with duets; he on the violin and she on the piano. I still vividly recall their rendition of Brahm's *Hungarian Dance* which was "something else".

Levi had a shop at No. 8 John Street, Waterford, where he dealt in furniture and antiques and did good business. My father told me that when the Levi's came to Waterford and took the shop at No. 8, they had with them a very old man, probably the uncle of his wife, and he carried on the business of money lending. As part of that business he used to buy gold sovereigns and half sovereigns and it was known that he would pay one pound and sixpence for a sovereign and ten shillings and threepence for a half sovereign. These coins were solid gold, with a milled edge, and were worth one pound, and ten shillings respectively. The sovereign weighed one fine ounce while the half sovereign was half a fine ounce. At that time all precious metals were measured in "Troy Weight".

Now this old man could be seen daily sitting in a rocking chair, in the window of the furniture shop, holding in his hands a small Buckskin bag and shaking it constantly as he rocked to and fro. It was this practice that earned him the nickname

"The Miser". The street urchins and indeed many adults used to congregate outside the shop and could be heard saying "see how he loves his money, even the sound of it jingling in his money bag." They could not have guessed the old man's secret!

My father explained it to me as an object lesson to illustrate the acumen of the Jewish businessman. Apparently the old man collected the gold coins for a particular purpose. When he had collected whatever he considered to be a sufficient number of

them he put them in the small leather bag and shook them for, let us say a week. Then at the end of that time, when he emptied out the coins, there remained in the bag a residue of gold dust. This happened because the milled edges of the coins rubbing against each other, when the bag was shaken, resulted in tiny flakes of gold coming off each coin. The real beauty of this procedure was that when fifty coins went into the bag the same fifty came out again and the deposit of gold dust, however small, was a net profit. So, to quote my father, you *can* have your cake and eat it … if you know how!

This story, which is true, instilled in me a very healthy respect for Jewish businessmen which has remained with me to this day.

The Rules (Woodstown)
Of Pitch And Toss
And How To Play It

1933

1. Any number can play, but six was considered a mini-
    mum because each player's stake was two pennies
    (pre-decimal) and six would provide a "pot" of one
    shilling.
2. Select a level piece of ground – soft clay or sandy – out
    of the breeze as cross winds can affect play.
3. Select a pyramid shaped stone about an inch high and
    inch and a half at the base and place it on the ground.
    It must sit firmly on its base and the ground around it
    should be worked over to a depth of a quarter inch or
    so. The idea here is that when a penny is pitched to

land near this stone it will not bounce but stick where it lands. The stone is known a *"The Motty"*.

4. A tall man must now mark off seven paces from the Motty to "the line".

5. Each player now stands in turn at the line and pitches *one penny* to the Motty.

6. When all the players have done this the nearness of each penny to the Motty determines the order in which the player will pitch and each player is numbered.

7. Now the game proper begins:- each player goes to the line by number and pitches two pennies to the Motty. The one nearest the Motty is left on the ground and the other one is picked up by the umpire or "purser" who stands by the Motty.

8. When all the players have pitched it is mutually decided by nearness of penny to the Motty which player is 1st, 2nd, 3rd, 4th, etc.

9. All the pennies are now picked up by the purser and handed to the player who is "first".

10. Now comes the vital part – the tossing! The player who is first places two pennies on a match box held between finger and thumb (the harp side must be facing upwards) and tosses them over his head so that they spin to the ground. Any penny which lands "head" side up he keeps and those which land "harp" side up

are handed on to the player who is second and so on till there are no pennies left and the game goes on to the next round the players keeping the same order as in 6.

Notes

- To play the game today, use a 2p coin – it is nearest in size to the old penny.
- Some players would not uses a match box to toss, preferring to use the flat of 2 fingers or a flat piece of stick called a *"Fecker"* (for "feckin' 'em" up in the air!).
- When there was a really big school – maybe 30 men – kids and sometimes men who literally did not have two pennies, would stand in the crowd near the Motty and when a penny would "go astray" or if an argument got going about the position of the pennies, our friend would put his foot down on the delinquent coin and stand his ground for a while. Then he would quietly inch to the back of the crowd, hopefully bringing the penny with him, when he could quickly bend down and pocket it. If a fellow could do this twice, he could have the stake of 2 pence to join in the game. This dodge was known as *"Stooping"* and may have been the origin of the question "how could one stoop so low?" The penalty for a stooper would be unpleasant!!
- "Arguing the toss" also came from this game.

Woodstown In The 1930s

1933

Pitch and Toss was a very popular pastime with country folk in the 30's and schools were to be seen at cross roads, especially in summer.

Here are the names of some of the men who used to gather at The Gap, The Chains, or Barron's Gates to chat on a Sunday and play pitch and toss or cards – the location depended on which way the wind was blowing.

Jimmy Hayes	Car driver	The Strand
Maurice Toole	Co. Council Road worker	Ballyglan Cottage
Pat Ivory (Feck)	Farmer's son	Ballyglan
Jack Power (Stretch)	Lorry Driver	Cooltegan
Benny Power	Farmer's son	Cooltegan
Martin Lynch	Farm worker & poacher	Dromina

Stephen Connolly	Farm worker & poacher	Dromina
Ned Leahy	Farm worker & well digger	Dromina
Stephen Dwyer	Farm worker & strong man	Dromina
Mikey Whelan	Home from England	Glenbower
Barney Whelan	Postman's son	Glenbower
Billy Whelan	Groom	Glenbower
Pat Kennedy	Road worker	Kilcop
Larry Fowler	Cottager with wooden leg	Rossduff
Tom Reidy	Farm worker	Rossduff
Jack Lynch	Farmer's son	Harristown
Jack Roche (Count)	Farm worker	Harristown
Joe Toole	Farmer	Killea
Dick Delahunty	Farmer's son	Harristown
Neddy Hearne	Road Worker	Rossduff
Jimmy Hearne	Ned's young brother	Rossduff
Tom Hayes (Monkey)	Farmer's son	Ballyvoreen
Jimmy Kane (bought warts)	Farm worker	Ballinkina
Sonny Flanagan (Peep o' day)	Farm worker	Creaden
Jim Smelser	Farm worker	Creaden
Willie Hearne	Farmer's son	Knockaveelish
Maurice Morris (Mock)	Farmer's son	Harristown
Jim Morris	Farmer's son	Harristown
Billy Leahy	Farm Worker	Drumrusk
Pat Ivory	Farmer's son	Raheen
Denny Ivory	Farmer's son	Raheen
Mossy Colfer	Farmer's son	Geneva Barracks

Billy Coughlan	Farmer's son	Dromina
Tony Coughlan	Farmer's son	Dromina
Tommy Whelan	Weir Worker	Ballyglan
Davy Drohan	Weir Worker	Rossduff Road
Paddy Toole	Farm Worker	Glenbower
Maurice Toole	Farm Worker	Glenbower
Jamesy Redmond	OAP	Woodstown Village
Paddy Power (Foxy)	Farmworker	Woodstown Village
Geoff Power	Blacksmith	Woodstown Village
Tom Flanagan	Farmworker	Woodstown Village
Tom's brother (Mouler)	Farm Worker	Woodstown Village
Pierre Flanagan	Farm Worker	Ballygunner Village
Mikey Gough	Groom	Ballyglan Cottage
Martin Quilty	Motorman (Sir Robert's Chauffeur)	Ballyglan Cottage
Bobby Beamish	Farmer's son	Creaden
Johnny Beamish	Farmer's son	Creaden
Jimmy Elliot (Ellett)	Bus Driver	Geneva Barracks?
Anthony Flanagan	Farm Worker	Creaden?
Jim Connors	Groom	Rossduff
Ned Connors	Farm worker	Rossduff
Jimmy Boland (Tarrier)	Road worker	Knockaveelish
Jack Boland	Huntsman	Knockaveelish
Mikey Boland	Farm worker	Knockaveelish
Jimmy Dunne	Farm worker	Woodstown Village
Billy Lucas (Boundary Bill)	Farm worker	Ballygunner
Mikey Moloney	Salmon weir worker	Raheen

Woodstown Cricket Club

1933

Woodstown cricket pitch was situated about a ¼ mile from the beach on the left hand side of the road to Waterford. The field itself was owned by Sir Robert Paul's family (I believe), or perhaps the estate of Winston Barron – memory fails me here. Anyway, it was mowed and rolled regularly and was as level as a billiard table.

According to the cricket moguls of the time it was "the best pitch in Europe" and was "nice and springy" and in no way "dead to the ball" and "sure wasn't there a good reason for everything, because at the time the pitch was laid there was an oul' galleon ran aground on Woodstown strand and didn't they bury the wreck under the cricket pitch and so 'tis no wonder it's nice and springy". Make what you like of that fable – perhaps wreckers of the time buried their evidence there – but it was without doubt a beautiful pitch.

I recall that there were matches there most Sundays during the summer and it was *the* place to go. All the locals would watch standing on the roadside ditch and those with no interest in the game could see everybody who was coming and going to beach.

Those who had cars – the secretary, Mr. O'Meara, had a Morris Cowley two-seater with a "dickey seat" in the back – would drive into the field and park to face the action. Their ladies, meantime, would be in the marquee setting up the tea for the teams.

Scorekeepers would sit on rugs at vantage points at the boundaries marking their (very detailed) score sheets and girls (who had the makings) would saunter along, from the gate to the far end of the field and back, pretending to be in deep conversation while they posed and covertly watched the reactions from the assembled gathering. It was really *the* place to be on your new bicycle.

The last time I looked into that field it was ploughed and harrowed and a crop of corn was peeping through the sod. I thought with great affection of all the lovely days I had there and I could almost hear the crowd cheering as Boundary Bill drove a ball over the trees at the far side of the road. I was on a sort of boy's team, being two years younger than my brother Dick, who was the youngest ever to get on the men's team.

Woodstown Cricket Club –
Some members 1934 approx.

Michael O'Meara	Polebery, Waterford	Dental Mechanic
J. L. Dempster	Waterford	Manager, Flour Mills
Sir Ernest Goff	Newtown, Waterford	Landowner
Oswald Hennesey	Dunmore East	Rep.
Bob Christie	Waterford	Bank Clerk
Mikey Nugent	Ballinkina, Rosduff	Farmer
Neddy Hearne	Rossduff Cross	Road Worker
Dick Cronin	Woodstown	Schoolboy
Billy Lucas	Ballygunner (Boundary Bill)	Farm Worker
Joe Toole	Killea	Farmer (?)
Jimmy Kane	Ballinkina	Farm Worker
Jimmy Whelan	Ballygunner	Haulier
Eddie Walsh	Waterford (The Knacker man)	

There was also a cricket club in Killea (Dunmore East) and another at Faithlegg (Passage East) and when important matches occurred members from one area frequently helped to defend the honour of neighbouring clubs.

> ### *Descriptions of a thin man:*
> *"You'd find more meat on the shin of a wren."*
> *"He's about as fat as a hen across the forehead."*
> *"You'd see more meat on a hammer!"*

The Art Of Making Snares

1934

When I was a boy, seventy years ago, rabbits were as plentiful in the countryside as seagulls at the seaside. They were a valuable source of food for poor people – at a time when work was scarce and badly paid and Social Welfare was non-existent. If you didn't have work you went hungry, or depended on the charity of neighbours, unless you had a bit of land on which to grow things to eat or to sell.

The famous Mrs. Beeton's instructions in her cookery book on how to make rabbit stew began with "First catch your rabbit", and the methods for so doing were varied. To hunt them with dogs, you needed two, first a terrier to flush them out of the thickets, and then a fast dog to take them on the run. The latter would be a whippet, or a lurcher, which was a cross between a greyhound and a collie, or indeed any kind of mongrel that could run faster than a rabbit. If you had money, you could buy a ferret (Ten Shillings) and a run of purse-nets for sixpence each, or a hank of netting twine and make the nets yourself. Gin traps were often used too, but most people felt they were a cruel method. Last on the list was a snare, made by twisting together several strands of fine brass wire, and making a lasso. This would be set in the path used by a rabbit, and secured with stout string to a peg driven into the ground beside the rabbit run. When the rabbit ran down his path, his head went through the noose and he was held fast until the owner of the snare came at dawn and put him in his bag.

Making the snare was a vital part of the operation and as a boy fond of hunting I longed to know exactly how to make them. I had visions of catching rabbits for the pot or maybe even selling them for sixpence each as some of the locals did.

In my quest for this vital knowledge, I met with Jack, a casual farm worker who had nine children. It was well known that they practically lived on rabbits, and that Jack was the expert on anything to do with hunting, including making snares. He took me with him a few times into the depths of the local woodlands, where he marked some likely rabbit runs suitable for laying snares. On one of these occasions a rabbit jumped out of a grass clump and had run about fifteen yards when Jack, without hesitation threw his stick and knocked him stone dead. On the way back, I asked Jack if he could teach me how to make a snare. I wasn't prepared for his answer.

"If you're going to first Mass in Crooke next Sunday, bring a coil of wire and a few eyelets with you, and I'll show you. The shop that sells the wire has the eyelets as well."

I agreed, and promised to meet him but wasn't quite clear on exactly the how and where. Anyway, I got the wire for sixpence and the eyelets for tuppence, I put the lot in my back pocket where my jacket would cover it, and got the bus to Mass at 8 a.m. that Sunday with my family.

There was no sign of Jack in the chapel yard when my family and I arrived and as we entered the chapel I mentally wrote off the whole thing, telling myself that adults didn't always keep their promises.

The stairs to the gallery, where my family always sat, had a landing, where a stained glass window was set into the wall. It was there that I found Jack, ensconced on the deep window ledge with the sun shining in on his back.

He beckoned me to sit beside him. I hung back a bit as the rest of my family went on up to the gallery. Once they were out of sight of us I sat in on the ledge with him and whispered "What about the snares?" He smiled and said "At the first stand up," and put his finger to his lips.

I knew what he meant, but I doubt, dear reader, that you will, so perhaps I should explain. The men at that time went to

Mass on a Sunday largely because their women folk insisted, or had to be ferried there, or because the priest would find out if they didn't, or because of what people might think. Anyway, it was a chance to meet other locals and have a chat before, after, and sometimes, during Mass. In general, they were quite removed from the liturgy, and hence the gospel was known as "the first stand up", followed by "the little sit down", and when the priest entered the pulpit for the sermon, that was "the big sit down" and could last for half an hour. But I digress!

The mighty hunter.
Circa 1930

Now, I handed the wire and the eyelets to Jack and he uncoiled a couple of feet of the wire. Then he took a three-inch nail out of one jacket pocket, and a round stone, the size of a goose egg, out of the other one. Next he took an eyelet and slipped it onto the nail, the point of which he stuck quietly into the window sill. He held the nail upright and as the congregation shuffled to its feet with the usual coughing and general noise, Jack hit the nail with the stone, driving it well into the wood. The sound was just like an iron-shod heel striking one of the metal brackets which secured the pews.

Jack then looped coils of wire around the eyelet on the nail whispering "Four strands for a rabbit, five for a hare, and six for a fox. Remember that."

The loops of wire were about a foot long and having snapped the wire, a second nail was inserted in the free end, and I was told to twist it. I did so and in minutes, I had a miniature wire rope with an eyelet at one end. Both nails were withdrawn and the small end put through the eyelet to make a perfect noose. At the "big sit down", the performance was repeated, and by the time the sermon was over, I had two perfect snares, which I hid under my jacket for the bus trip home.

I caught many a fine rabbit with those two snares and many others which I made with my new-found know-how, and I never forgot Jack and his kindness in showing a little boy the tricks of the trade.

Jack disappeared soon afterwards, and I heard that he had "taken the boat", and gone to England to provide for his family. Oddly enough, I remember best the smell of his pipe, which he smoked whenever he had the price of a plug of tobacco.

❧

Description of a guy who had a prominent chin:
"He has a chin fit to poke a cat from under a bed!"

How the Stable Was Built

1936

Mick and his wife Peg lived at the top of Failun (pronounced Falloon) hill, on the road which went from Hickey's Cross in Rosduff to the Fairy Bush in Killea. They occupied a "labourer's cottage" with a half acre at the back and the rent was ten pence per week.

Mick had injured his leg some years before and that leg was slightly shorter than the other one and he walked with the aid of a stick. Because of his disability, Mick was virtually unemployable, since the only work available in the area was of the labouring variety.

Over the years he had scraped together the price of a black ass – two pounds – and a trap, which went for thirty shillings at an executor's sale, came his way the following year. Thus equipped, Mick was able to earn a shilling or two doing errands, to and from the Gaultier Creamery Shop, for neighbours. Apart from that he spent most of his time tending that part of the half acre which wasn't set aside for the ass to graze.

Peg hired out as a charlady, at two shillings per day, to any lady who needed her services and it was on that basis that my mother took her on to do cleaning, washing, ironing and general housework at our home in Woodstown. She would walk the two and a half miles to our home and arrive at eight thirty on the dot – and always in the best of spirits. She had never been to school and could neither read nor write but she was an absolute mine of information on all matters relating to country living and survival. One of her great goals in life was that she an Mick might live to draw an old-age-pension – it was five shillings a week then, and a dog license cost the

Our charlady with her husband (The Man), the famous ass plus my younger brother & sister David and Claire & friends -1933

same amount! Incidentally, Peg always referred to her husband as *The Man* and the locals always knew him by that name.

My mother enjoyed Peg's company, not just because Peg never arrived empty handed – she would always bring a few fresh mushrooms, or a can of blackberries, or a small bunch of wild flowers. This woman had a generous heart and my mother appreciated that fact. She loved music and my mother would switch on the radio when Peg arrived and both of them would enjoy that continuous programme called "Music While You Work", which was a ploy used by the BBC to keep the factories of England going at top speed during the war.

Come lunchtime, Mother would sit down with Peg and get all the gossip and on one such day she said to Peg "I'll just switch off the wireless while we have our lunch."

"Oh, yes," said Peg "let the poor fellows off to their lunch – they've been playin' there all mornin'!"

On her day with us Peg's husband, *The Man*, would arrive about four o'clock with the ass & trap, to bring Peg home. While he waited for her to finish he would tether the ass and head off into the woods to collect a "bearth" of sticks to take home for the fire.

Mick had a wealth of songs, which he would sing in a sort of monotone, and also a repertoire of poems and country stories. As kids, we loved the songs best. Titles like "Pat Hegarty's Auld Brother's Britches", "Workin' on the Railway, "Toora Loora Loo" and "The Monkey Married the Baboon's Sister" intrigued us no end.

The man was making plans to build a stable for the ass, he told us, and when we saw him cutting some nice straight poles in the wood he told us that these were to make the frame of the stable. This frame would be covered with iron sheets he said and we wondered how this might come about. In the event the solution was a composite one. First of all the man visited all the sites where road works were taking place and he bought all the empty tar barrels for sixpence each and ferried them home in the trap. When he thought he had enough – it took two months to collect a sufficient number – he set about removing the bottoms and lids using a hammer and cold chisel. He finished this stage by opening up the side seams, and then he waited.

Almost a month passed by before a day arrived when the steam-roller came over the top of the hill and approached the man's cottage. Mick hailed the driver, whom he knew well, and when the roller stopped he got the road workers to spread the opened up barrels on the road. Whereupon the driver took his steam-roller over and back across the barrels until they were quite flat. Then the road workers brought the "sheets" into Mick's yard, where they were thanked. The man had the covering for his stable which he duly nailed to the frame, making sure to put them on with the tarry side up! This dodge would save painting the stable as it would be tarred all over and waterproof.

One of the local stories which *The Man* had was about an old church ruin which was situated in a field near his cottage. Apparently the church had been torn down during the time of the Penal Laws and one of the holy water fonts had survived.

The legend was that if you had warts on your hand you only had to dip the hand in the dew that collected in the font and say three Hail Marys and the warts would disappear.

Now I had a massive wart on the ring finger of my left hand and couldn't get rid of it, no matter what I did. I tried all the known "cures", like dandelion juice, rubbing it with a snail and sticking him on a thorn bush, etc. etc. These "cures" had no effect and in desperation I decided to try the holy water font in the ruined church, although to be honest I didn't really believe in it.

Mick agreed to show me where the ruin was – he did believe – and informed me that part of the ritual was that I should go up there on foot, no manner of transport was allowed. This meant a walk of almost three miles there and another three miles back and this was a daunting pilgrim- age for a boy of ten.

I thought about it for a week or so and eventually decided to "go for it." On the appointed day I set off early, having arranged for a pal to join me. We arrived, very tired, at Mick's cottage at about mid-day. We accomplished the final leg of the journey and when Mick pointed out the ruin I went in unaccompanied and dipping in my afflicted hand I said the prayers.

On the way back to Mick's house, I decided secretly that I would watch my wart day and night and never take my eyes off it, to see if anything would happen, and I told no one about this dark secret.

We got a cup of tea at Mick's and he told us it was not mandatory to walk back and he very kindly tackled up the ass & trap and drove us home, much to our relief.

Now to this day I cannot explain just why I forgot to watch that wart, but forget I did. My previous obsession with the wart just evaporated and when I did remember to look, about a week later… the wart was *GONE* and no trace of it remained. I swear that this is true but don't ask me how or why – I just wasn't looking!

By the way, seventy years later, I should tell you that it never did come back!!

> ## Propositions made by a farmer
> ## to a prospective labourer.
> 1. *I'll give ye ten shillin's a week and I'll ate, or fifteen shillin's and ate yerself*
> 2. *Ten shillin's a week and the run of yer gums.*
> 3. *Ten shillin's a week and yer peck.*

The Devil Finds Work

1936

It was the week before midsummer's day and the farm yard was baking in the early afternoon sun.

The town boy cycled slowly through the big yard gate and freewheeled down the sloping yard, past the cattle pens on one side and the big hay-shed on the other, through the arch under the corn loft and stopped by the dairy. Here he dismounted and dropped his sweet can on the steps of the dairy. It was a new, shiny can with a wire handle and although carefully washed by his mother, it still smelled of the boiled sweets which it originally contained. Now, however, it was used for the daily collection of six pints of milk from the farm.

Sweet cans were very much part of life in those days. Boiled sweets were made in Hartreys Sweet Factory at the apple market in Waterford and they were packed in tin cans holding five or six pounds weight for dispatch to the shops. Shopkeepers would sell the can when empty for sixpence or might even give one free to a good customer. In any event, they were in common use in the country for carrying milk, water from the well, blackberries, mushrooms, cockles from the beach, butter, nails for building, lugworms for fishing and anything else you could think of.

Now the town boy sat by his can on the steps of the dairy facing the back door of the house where the scotch cattle dog dozed in the shade. The dog hadn't moved for he knew the boy well and was used to seeing him come to the dairy and wait there for Kevin, the farmer's young son.

The boy did not dream of approaching the back door to "call" for his friend because inside that kitchen dwelt Katty, the housekeeper, and she ruled with an iron hand. She had big feet with boots like a man, an apron made from a cotton flour bag and her hair, which fascinated the boy, was plaited at either side of her head and the plaits were then coiled up over her ears like black headphones. Her heavy unsmiling mouth showed a front tooth missing and her voice was like the crack of a whip.

Katty, a faithful retainer of the family, was regarded by the boys as a "murderous oul' bitch", in private of course, but the truth was that she catered for a family of nine plus four farm hands, saw to the calves, made the butter, cured the bacon and baked the bread and, as a kind of recreation, she looked after the fowl, her pride and joy.

With the work load she had, Katty was quick to grab

any bit of help she could and Kevin was constantly being "nailed" to carry buckets to the calves or feed the dogs or turn the handle of the butter churn or bring in water from the pump or any one of a hundred other chores which so often kept him from joining his pal.

The town boy resented her, for he was hungry for company and loved everything about the huge farm and the fun he and Kevin had when they got together. For a town boy it was heaven – peeping in at the massive bull, diving from the top of the hay in the shed into the loose hay below, dipping apples into the cream bucket in the dairy and harpooning imaginary whales with hay pikes. It was the kind of magic which only ten-year-olds can weave.

As the town boy sat there, thinking of what he and Kevin might do and wondering how soon his pal might appear, two of the farm hands walked by on their way out to the fields and their rough voices cut through his thoughts.

"…an' when I was puttin' out the cows this mornin' there was a big vixen standin' at the orchard gate lookin' in at the hens in the haggert," said Mossy.

"Jazes boy," said Stephen, "I'd say she have cubs above in the corrig and with the rabbits gone scarce there now she'll be down after Katty's hens any minute."

"Begod, Mossy, ye're right," said the other man, "I'll tell Katty to tie the dog in the haggert for a few nights an' maybe the boss would give you the gun in the mornin' when ye're goin' for the cows."

The two men passed the boy, engrossed in their talk,

and paid him no heed, but he pondered their conversation and all that it entailed and marvelled at the thought that one hungry fox could cause so many problems in the farm.

When Kevin appeared, it was an hour to milking time and they set off up to the big hay shed chatting like a pair of magpies.

In the shed they climbed the ladder to the top of the first bench of hay and scrambled up the rest of the way to the top. There they could touch the hot iron roof and they lay down on their bellies and peeped down into the haggert where the hens were picking about the place and clucking quietly among themselves. They were coming in from the orchard in twos and threes now, as feeding time approached and soon Katty would be along with her bucket of scraps and a scoop of grain to feed them and talk to them like children.

Suddenly the town boy sat up, his eyes dancing.

"D'ye know what I heard a man telling my father last night?"

"What," said Kevin.

"Well," giggled the boy, "he said that if you got a hen and put her head under her wing and swung her from side to side seven times the hen would go fast asleep."

Kevin hooted with laughter and so did his pal and they rolled around in the hay till they were out of breath. As they sat up facing each other and the laughter was about to erupt again, Kevin said, "Hey, I wonder if it works?"

There was a silence for just a moment, then the pair slid down to the first bench an dived to the bottom.

It took a bit of running before they caught the hen and she squawked loudly as Kevin held her up. Then the town boy grabbed her head, lifted her wing, pushed her head under and lowered the wing to enclose the head. Kevin held her in front of him like a rugby ball, a hand on each wing.

"Come on," hissed the town boy, "swing her." Kevin did so and they counted together as the bird was swung side to side, three, four, five, six, seven. Kevin stopped. The bird was limp in his hands.

"Look at her legs hangin' down," said the town boy, wonder in his voice. "Jazes Kevin, she's asleep. It works."

Kevin laid the hen down on its belly and they both looked at it. It didn't move.

"Oh Jazes," said Kevin, "maybe she's smothered."

The town boy poked the hen and she rolled on her side. He gently touched the wing and out slid the hen's head. Her eyes opened and she fluttered up with a loud squawk and ran off down the haggert. The two sat on the ground in silence, their boy's minds racing with the enormity of their discovery…and the possibilities it opened up, and, as they looked at each other, the town boy reached out and took his pal by the sleeve,

"What d'ye say, Kevin," he grinned, "if we catch all the hens and put 'em to sleep all around the haggert before Katty comes up to feed 'em?"

"Oh Jazes," said Kevin, his eyes widening, "she'll think they're dead or something." They laughed as they herded a bunch of hens into an empty stall and closed the door. One by one they brought the sleeping hens out and laid them about the haggert, all on their sides with the head underneath so that they couldn't wake up.

They had just put out number fourteen when they heard Katty starting up from the kitchen with her bucket. They barely had time to get to the top of the hay in the shed before she arrived. They peeped down to watch from the safety of their hiding place.

The hens who were not asleep heard Katty too and started to run towards her as she headed up into the haggert. They reminded the town boy of the men who took part in the fathers' race at the school sports.

Katty was crooning her usual "chook, chook, chook," as she rounded the corner, her hand in the bucket to scatter the food. She looked up, stopped and dropped the bucket, her mouth open as she gazed around at the scene of carnage.

"Aw Jesus, God," she wailed, "me lovely hens, God curse an' blast that hoor's melt of a fox. He's after eatin' the heads off all me lovely hens.

Donny, Donny, come boy," she yelled, summoning the big cattle dog.

"Mikey, get the gun quick," she howled, "the fox is in the haggert. Help, help," she cried at the top of her voice, "the fox, the fox."

Everyone seemed to arrive together: the dog and Mikey, Mossy, and Simon who were on their way in for the milking when they heard the shouting. They were all looking at Katty, her face tear stained and her eyes blazing.

"Can't ye see what's after happenin'," she bawled, "lookit me hens, will ye. Can't ye go and get the bastard fox and don't be standin' there," and she bent down to pick up the nearest "body".

The hen fluttered awake and ran off squawking. The colour drained from Katty's face as she touched the next corpse which also woke. The men began to titter as Katty gave the next one a savage kick, causing it a rude awakening. And on she went, wielding her big boots in a service of resurrection while her audience howled with laughter and ribbed her unmercifully.

Katty glowered at them all, picked up her bucket, wiped her nose with the tail of her apron and started back towards the house. The laughter tapered off and Mossy ventured, "Shure, I'd say this was only the young fellas that done it for divilment, Katty."

"Well," said Katty, quietly, "we'll see about that." She was standing by the dairy now, looking at the town boy's bike and his sweet can, Then she headed for the kitchen door, calling over her shoulder, "'Tis milking time, get in the cows."

The two culprits had cleared out fast when the first hen woke, slipped out on the yard side of the hayshed, down the back avenue into the meadow beyond where they laughed and rolled about in the grass, mimicking Katty in her distress, and hooting with laughter till their sides were sore. Afterwards they went on down the strand where they re-enacted whole charade, taking it in turns to be Katty and using piles of seaweed as the sleeping hens. Finally they headed back towards the farm, flushed and tired.

The milking was over and they could see the cows on the hill road going back to the fields. The town boy knew it was time to collect his can of milk an' get home for tea and Kevin had decided to get back into the house through the orchard door before Katty got back from the dairy. It was her practice to supervise the milking, see the various churns and cans filled correctly and separate the cream before tea time.

The town boy eased his way through the wicket gate behind the calf house and peeped round the corner. His milk can was filled and ready on the trestle table by the dairy door. He could hear Katty inside washing the separator cups and laying them out to dry on the butter table. He walked quietly to his bike and wheeled it over to the table. He reached out quickly, gripped the wire handle of the can for a quick lift and an even quicker getaway. For some unknown reason, however, the handle came adrift at one side and six pints of milk hit him on the chest, soaking him clear to the soles of his feet. In the process he fell over and the bike landed on top of him.

He looked up to find Katty standing over him, reaching down to lift the bike and, as he stole a sidelong glance at her face, he could see the gap in her teeth. She was actually smiling!

"Mossy," she commanded, "bring up a clean sack here, the poor little townie fella is afther drowndin' himself with the milk." Mossy obeyed and helped the lad up, wiping him vigorously with a rough, musty grain sack.

"Aw, begod," he said, "ye'll hafta learn how to lift a can of milk if ye're to live in the country." He laughed as the boy began to squelch about in the milk filled shoes, trying to pull the wet clothes out from his body. Katty was laughing too and Simon and Mikey came on the scene and gave the boy a cruel, country ribbing.

Quite suddenly, Katty said, "that'll do ye now, get on about yeer bisiness the lot of ye," and, to the boy, "come in here, child, till I fix that can and fill it for ye."

With that, she took a pliers from the pocket of her apron and deftly closed the loop at the end of the handle and clipped it in place.

"Get on yer bike now, and I'll hand ye the can in case ye'd spill it again," she said. The town boy did as he was bid.

"Thanks, Katty," he said quietly, very close to tears now and, as he looked at her, he thought her hard features softened a little as she said, "Go on now boy and I hope yer mother won't be too hard on ye."

He cycled slowly out the gate and as he freewheeled towards home he kept getting this picture of Katty taking the pliers from her apron pocket. He was in sight of his own gate when it dawned on him.

"The bloody oul bitch, "he whispered to himself, "she did it on me. There was nothing wrong with that can at all. She doctored the handle on purpose" ...and he still had his mother to face!

What followed when the town boy got home is best forgotten. Suffice it to say that words like 'Amadan' and 'butterfingers' were used and his brother gave him a proper roasting particularly since an examination of the can revealed no fault in the handle. The boy went to bed sore and sorry for himself.

In the farmhouse tea time came and as the table filled up Simon asked Mossy if he had remembered to leave the alarm clock in the haggert to wake the hens in the morning. Laughter exploded and Mikey capped Simon by saying that today should be known as the Day of the Headless Hens. More laughter ensued which Katty ignored and, as she began to cut more cake bread, she conjured up for them the misfortunes of the little town boy.

Mossy chimed in with "Begod 'twas funny alright when he stood up and the milk spurted up out of his shoes." Kevin laughed as loudly as the rest, though he felt a twinge of uneasiness he could not quite explain.

Kevin went to bed early that night, partly because he was tired, but also to keep out of Katty's way, just in case of repercussions.

He woke next morning to her usual call, "Come on, Kevin, breakfast!" He stepped out of bed, straight down on a sharp pebble. The pain was savage and he hopped about holding his foot, only to land on another pebble. He yelled in pain, hopping and jumping about and landing on a pebble every other time. Eventually he got out on to the landing, crying with pain and trying to hold both aching feet at once. Katty came up the stairs two at a time, shouting as she came.

"What in God's name are ye doin' Kevin?" She got to the landing and the tearful lad pointed to the bedroom floor, littered with pebbles.

"They fell out of yer pockets when you were undressing I suppose, come on now, stop yer bawlin' and dress yerself," and, as she went downstairs, her final words came faintly, "maybe somebody put 'em there for a joke."

"Some friggin' joke," said Kevin, trying to put a foot under him. It hurt!

The whole breakfast table had heard the story by the time Kevin appeared and everybody laughed and poked fun at him about it. He didn't rightly know which hurt most, his pride or his feet, and when he saw Katty absently fishing three pebbles out of her apron pocket with the comment "them little stones seem to be everywhere today" he almost choked as he realised the truth of what had happened.

It was a very chastened town boy who arrived at the dairy step that afternoon and he was joined by an equally quiet, almost sullen, Kevin and they wandered up to the hayshed discussing their respective tales of woe and wondering what else was to come. They both agreed that they had tangled with a force much greater than their own and with far, far more expertise and finesse.

"Jazes boy," said Kevin," we should never have done that with the poor oul' hens."

"I know," said the town boy, "Katty loves every one of 'em like they were children."

"And did ye see the state she got into when she thought they were dead?" Said Kevin. "'Twas like hell at a wake." The town boy nodded, and they fell silent, sitting in the hay. They never heard Katty coming into the shed till she spoke.

"Come on you two," she said, "in to the kitchen. I want to talk to ye."

They followed her in, eyeing each other fearfully. She closed the door behind them and the two sat together on the big furrim behind the table, backs to the wall, looking small and nervous.

Katty picked up a huge knife and quickly cut two long slices off a fresh soda cake and spread them with salty butter and newly made gooseberry jam. Next she poured two mugs of tea and laced them with plenty of milk and three spoons of sugar each. She began to talk quietly and as she talked she moved the feast towards the two boys.

"I was wonderin'," said she slowly, "if ye'd agree with somethin' I read there a while ago about practical jokes. It was this fella was sayin' that practical jokes are great fun for everybody, except the one havin' the joke played oh him. What would ye say to that now?"

"I'd say 'twas the truth," said the town boy.

"An I'd say the man was right too," said Kevin without hesitation.

"Well," said Katty, "I was thinkin' the same meself. Now, let ye ate up and drink up and be out of my kitchen in five minutes."

The boys needed no second invitation, but grabbed the delicious bread and sucked up the sweet tea gratefully and exchanged a meaningful glance over the top of the steaming mugs.

Katty turned her back and pretended to poke the fire.

A small farmer engaged to be married to a very plain looking, but wealthy, girl was asked if he couldn't have got a prettier prospect. He replied –

"Well, I reckoned that a bit of money never spoiled a good lookin' girl."

The Financier

and The Farmer's Wife

1936

Smullian was a Jew who lived in Parnell Street when I was a boy. His wife was by way of being a very good singer and featured in the Wallace Grand Opera Society which had been thriving there in my father's time.

Smullian had a brass plate on the outside of his front door which glittered and said "J. SMULLIAN. FINANCIER". In fact, he had a money lending business and he also bought and sold "job" lots of groceries and salvage from marine claims which arose in the port from time to time – there was a considerable cargo trade in and out of Waterford Port in those years.

The money-borrowing clients, mostly poor people, would not necessarily be in the market to buy salvage goods from

Smullian, but he was well known among the farming people of the outlying areas who came to town once a week to sell their butter and eggs and were always on the lookout for a bargain of any kind.

Cute farmers, and the equally cute wives of these cute farmers, were known to have dealings with Mr. Smullian from time to time, and it was generally agreed that "he'd have the odd bargain, alright".

One such lady from the agricultural community dropped in to Smullian's office about mid-day on a Saturday, after selling her butter in High Street Market. It was a casual visit to see if he had anything interesting to sell, or rather to see if he had anything at all useful at an interesting price.

Smullian treated his client with the utmost deference, he informed her that he had a consignment of Dutch matches, which he fully recommended and she could have a packet of twelve boxes for ninepence, saving a massive $33^1/_3$ percent on shop prices. She looked at the open sample box carefully. She knew, of course, that anything coming from a foreign place could be suspect, but they had good strong stems and fat round heads and she plunged.

"Ninepence it is" she said counting out three coppers and a sixpenny bit and she put the packet in her basket, covering it carefully with newspaper so that "nobody would know her business".

Now, threepence may not sound much of a saving to you, my dear reader, but you should know that at that time, potatoes sold for sixpence a stone (14 pounds), a seat in the cinema was fourpence, and you could buy five Woodbine cigarettes for two pence, or four apples for a penny. So, a woman who saved threepence on one transaction, could well feel pleased with herself.

This particular lady was well pleased as she drove home to her little farmhouse with her husband in their pony and trap. She had already decided to buy another dozen boxes of these matches next Saturday, and that would see her through the winter months. She had also decided to say nothing to her neighbour 'till the week after, when maybe they'd be all gone.

Eight o'clock mass that Sunday morning was in a cold church, two and a half miles drive from the farm, and it was near ten o'clock by the time they got home, and she knelt at the hearth to light the fire and put on the kettle for the tea. "Himself" was coming in after unyoking the pony when he heard his wife fervently cursing on her knees by the hearth.

"The divil blast that bloody Jewman for a swindlin' bastard" she ranted.

"Hauld on there girl" said himself, "what's wrong at all?"

"These God cursed Dutch matches won't light," she said, tears of rage and shame rolling down her face, for she had boasted of her bargain to her husband on the way home.

He picked up the box and tried to strike one. No good – another, the head crumpled – one more, not a spark. He put down the box, smiled indulgently at her, and said "you were codded girl" and handed her his own box of "decent" matches.

She lit the fire, got the breakfast, and life proceeded in the house. After the breakfast, she took the dozen packets of Dutch matches and placed them carefully on the chimney-breast, beside the picture of the Sacred Heart, and thought about next Saturday and her anger simmered.

When next Saturday came, she went to town as usual and on arrival she marched with resolute step to the door with the brass place which said J. Smullian, Financier. She went in and rapped on the little office counter.

As Smullian appeared, greeting her graciously, she slammed down the matches, which incidentally had dried off to perfection after spending the week on the chimney piece.

"Them matches are useless," she snapped. "They won't light and I wants me ninepence back, and I may say you have a neck to be coddin' decent people out of their hard earned money."

"Just a minute Ma'am" he said, totally ignoring the insult. "Let me see." He took up the nearest box and opened it taking out a match. He looked at it carefully, and then, lifting up his knee in front of him, he reached behind and swished the match swiftly along the underside of his buttock, the friction causing the match to light perfectly. He blew it out and took out another, and repeated the process, and again it lit. As he extinguished the third match, he closed the packet and moved it towards her with a smile.

"There's nothing whatever wrong with these matches, dear lady," he said "They light perfectly."

She reddened with anger and replied "It's all very well for you to say that Mr. Smullian, but where the hell do ye think I'm going to find a Jewman's arse at seven o'clock in the morning when I want to light a fire?"

I leave it to you to guess whether or not she recovered her ninepence!

Mikey was a very short man who rode a very old, very high bike. He was described by one of his colleagues as being –

"Like a cat up on a pair of scissors."

The Hound From Hell

1936

In the 1930s in Waterford there was a thriving Greyhound Racing Track and there were race meetings there once a week – sometimes twice. The sport was very popular in the City and County as there was a tradition of hare coursing and lots of people kept Greyhounds as a hobby.

The race meetings were great social occasions and owners from the surrounding counties of Kilkenny, Wexford and South Tipperary were to be seen there. Bookmakers from these places were also in evidence and the betting was always brisk. There was big money to be made at the track and, of course, lost too.

I had been taken to a few meetings and knew a lot of the owners who were from the City. In fact my father's bakery produced and sold toasted wholemeal rusks, which were popular as Greyhound feed. Chatting to the men who came to our shop to buy rusks meant that I was inevitably drawn closer to the Greyhound scene than might otherwise have been in the case, and the thought of owning my own hound began to take root in my mind. Of course, it was completely out of the question, even though I was then living in Woodstown, and often went hunting rabbits with my old mongrel dog.

Fate then took a hand when the clerk to a bookie, who was a regular at the track, died suddenly leaving a wife and two children. This man was well known and liked, and since life insurance was the exception rather than the rule at that time, the widow found herself in financial difficulty.

The response from his colleagues from "The Track" in general was prompt and generous. Various fund-raising events were staged to aid the family and one man donated a Greyhound which had a pedigree and papers to prove it. This dog was to be raffled and sure to raise a good sum of money for the cause. When I heard about the raffle, I bought two tickets and thought no more about it.

About a week later I happened to be staying at the shop overnight, when about midnight there was a loud knocking at the shop door. My father got up and went downstairs to find two men at the door looking for me, and they had a large Greyhound, which they said I had won in a raffle. To cap it all, one of the men offered me ten pounds on the spot if I would sell the dog. My father took me aside and said he thought I should accept, but I reasoned that if the dog was worth ten pounds in the middle of the night, he should be worth at least twice that in the morning. So, my father reluctantly agreed to leave it until tomorrow, and I put the dog in an outhouse and went back to bed.

Next day my father, who had looked over the dog's papers, suggested I should give him a trial on the track, see what time he made, and then decide what he might be worth. He also offered to pay the track fee for the test – three shillings and sixpence.

So off I went with my very own Greyhound in his new coat – it was navy edged with red – and swanky new collar and lead. On arrival at the track he was weighed – sixty pounds – paw printed, and got a registration card. Next he was put in the traps and the hare came flying around.

I watched to see that fawn coloured rocket shoot out and cover the 525 yards in 29+ seconds. But nothing happened when the trap opened. Then my "rocket" walked out, sat down and started to scratch his ear. I put him back in the trap and asked the guy to send the hare around again. He did so, and this time the dog didn't come out at all. He was asleep in the trap!!

It was suggested that I go around to the far side of the track and whistle the dog to see if he would run at all, and when I did this, he jumped the fence and cut across the football pitch which the track enclosed, and stood beside me wagging his tail. It was a disaster!

So I walked him back in all his finery and my father laughed and said "He may be well bred, but he's just not a tracker." I said I'd take him to Woodstown and use him to hunt rabbits, where he could at least earn his keep. I could not have been more wrong! When I took him out into a field with some of my pals and we put up a rabbit, he just looked at it and I had to unleash my mongrel, who promptly caught the rabbit. On taking him home, he strolled into the kitchen and swiped a whole pound of butter off the table and downed it in a minute. My mother had ructions and said "Don't let that hound in again." So, I shut the door, only to find that my friend stood on his hind legs and banged on the latch until it opened.

There followed a series of incidents which included his running the local Sergeant off the property. I was told to get rid of the dog – "immediately"!

Casting about for a suitable "victim", I asked a taxi man, whose brother had a farm, if he would take him, and I showed him the pedigree papers and the new coat, collar and lead to sweeten the deal. The taxi man took him and drove away, and "Captain" as I had called him, was out of my life.

A month later, I met the Taxi man and asked him how the dog was getting on, and he said that the day he let him out of the car in the brother's farmyard, he killed ten hens in less than five minutes, and his brother took out his gun and shot him dead before he could do any more damage. I was too shocked to say anything.

R.I.P. "Captain".

The Station

1936

In the combined parishes of Killea, Crooke and Faithlegg, when I was a boy, there was an event called "The Station". I never could find out why it had that name for it had nothing whatever to do with the railway, the nearest one being some ten miles away. In fact it was the term used in country places to describe a Mass which was said in a parishioners house each year – and it was a signal honour to have one's house selected by the Parish Priest for this purpose.

The venue would be announced at Sunday Mass and even that announcement was sufficient to establish one's status in the community. The particular areas to be "covered" by each Station would be decided by tradition – and probably influenced by the electoral register. The effect was that every person in every area, or at least the head of the household, would attend a Station Mass once a year and one of the objects of the exercise was that "dues" would be paid on that occasion.

The normal "dues" would be paid at the church door on a Sunday and the names of the contributors would be read from the altar AND the amounts contributed. The Station dues seemed, to my young mind at the time, to be an extra tax on a struggling rural community and the method used was a sort of "sweeper" arrangement to pick up the stragglers and squeeze the maximum out of the parish.

On the occasion of the Station, confessions would be heard and Mass would be said. Then, at the end of the mass, the priest produced his book, stood before the altar and called out the names of the parishioners. When your name was called you walked up to the priest, handed him your offering – in front of all your neighbours – and he would mark his book accordingly.

Although I was quite young, I was living in Woodstown when I first witnessed this procedure, I felt that it was demeaning and unfair. However, such was the standing of the clergy at the time that this process was accepted.

Another aspect of the Station was that people went to endless trouble and expense to "do up" the place in advance of the priest's visit. Farmhouses would be whitewashed; yards would be cleared of dung-heaps; cow-house doors would get a lick of paint; parlours would be freshly papered and have fires lit in them and, of course, children would be scrubbed clean and dressed in their Sunday clothes – all because of what the neighbours might think and so that they could hold their heads up going to mass on a Sunday and "nothing could be said!"

When it came to my family's turn to host the Station Mass I was eight or nine years old and I well recall the fuss that was created and how every corner of the house had to be completely cleaned. All the family got special assignments for the day: My sister was to answer the door and to show people into the drawing room; my younger brother had to make sure that the dogs were kept in the back yard and my mother was preparing a sumptuous breakfast in what we called the "sea parlour", which overlooked the beach.

My job was to light the fire in the drawing room, and to see that it was kept fed with coal and logs. The altar for the mass was set up in that room and I made sure that it was nice and warm.

When "the day" arrived it was cold and frosty and the ladies of the parish arrived in good time for the Mass and positioned themselves in a semicircle around the fire. The men hung around outside, smoking their Woodbines and chatting, as there would be no point going in until the priest arrived.

Meanwhile, my young brother, having secured the dogs, rambled in to see who had come. Peeping around the door jamb he beheld several ladies with their backs to the fire, skirts raised, toasting their bottoms! Having noted the colour of the "ample" knickers, he retreated silently and reported what he had seen to rest of us kids. Amid great whispering and sniggering the rest of us went in turns and gazed at this remarkable sight.

When we told my mother that we knew what colour knickers old Mrs. so & so was wearing she threatened us with hellfire and brimstone if we breathed a word of this to anyone. We retreated hastily from the kitchen but we could hear her laughing.

A story is told about a priest who was doing the Station Masses in his parish. He had developed a taste for Mustard and at that time mustard had hardly been heard of in country districts. It was the custom for the hostess of the Station Mass to provide an especially good breakfast for the priest and he could look forward to fresh eggs, home cured bacon, home made black & white puddings with fresh cake bread and strong tea. The only thing which might be missing from this princely spread would be – you've guessed it – a spot of mustard.

Well, you see, mustard wasn't really in general use and rather than embarrass the hostess by asking for something she didn't have the priest took the habit of carrying a small tin of mustard, ready mixed to his liking, in his pocket. So, if it came with the breakfast well & good, and if not he could discreetly use his personal supply.

It so happened, on this particular morning, that when the priest's breakfast was served there was no mustard to be seen on the table. Deciding to resort to subterfuge, he deliberately dropped his knife in the floor knowing that his hostess would fetch a fresh one from the kitchen, which she did. While she was out of the room the priest put a good dollop of his own cache on the side of his plate.

When the lady returned with the knife she looked at the priest's plate in absolute horror. She grabbed the plate and began to back out of the room saying "I'm awful sorry Father, them hens are everywhere. I'll get you a fresh breakfast!!"

So much for carrying your own supplies!

Describing a returned emigrant who had put on a lot of weight:

"He has a neck of meat on him like an American priest!"

The Price Of A Habit

1937

Birth and death are common events in the life of a farm and people of the land tend to be stoical about such matters. In the 1930s, farming where I lived was at a low ebb. Things were very tough on the land and you had to be tough in every respect to make any kind of living on a farm.

A farmer's wife had no soft options then. She worked in the house, lucky if she had water laid on, managed the family, the small yard animals, the dairy, the fowl and all produce from those areas. To her, a shilling was a shilling and if anyone knew the value of it in real terms, she surely did.

So it was, when her husband died and the priest and the doctor were gone, the woman tackled the pony and drove into town to complete the funeral arrangements. She stabled the pony in Dower's yard at the Car Stand and made her way up John St. to the far end of the Apple Market.

In the corner of the Market Square was Davey Power's Undertaking Establishment and Coffin Shop and, when he had sympathised with the widow, a price for the coffin of her choice was negotiated.

This done, she said, "Well now, Mr. Power, what are you going to charge me for a decent habit (shroud) to bury him in?"

"Five shillin's," he answered.

"Is that the best you can do, now, Mr. Power," she said, "and me buyin' the coffin an' all?"

"That would be the very best I could do, ma'am, for a good decent habit, "he replied, "an' you won't do better."

"Thanks, Mr. Power," she said, "but I'm goin' up the town and I think I'll do a lot better. I'll call in to ye on me way back."

Davy Power was "crabbed", as they say in Waterford, and sorely annoyed that his price should even be questioned.

After leaving the undertaker the woman went up Michael Street, round the corner to Patrick Street and into Veale's Drapery Shop where she purchased a habit of reasonable quality for three shillings and sixpence. She straightened her hat while waiting for her change, put the parcel containing the habit in her basket and set off again for the undertaker's.

As she turned the corner of the Apple Market she saw Davy standing outside the door of his shop, where it was nice and sunny, and she passed by the open hall doors where women were sweeping out their hallways and continuing with the brush across the pavement. There would be an audience for what followed!

Davy took the offensive as the woman drew near.

"Well ma'am," he said loudly, "were you able to get a cheap habit up the town?"

"Well," she echoed, just as loudly, "I got a very good habit in Veale's for three and sixpence an' it's every bit as good as what you offered me for five shillin's."

With that she handed him the parcel and turned on her heel. He would be out later to coffin the man.

Davy tore the parcel open and shook the garment out of its folds and looked at it, disdain on every line of his face.

"Alright, ma'am," he called after her, "but I must tell you this, his arse will be out through that in a week!"

> ### *Asked why he had never married, a country bachelor replied–*
> *"Why would I give away one half of me dinner to get the other half cooked?"*

The Gun

1938

When I was growing up, in Woodstown, Co. Waterford in the 1930s, my dream was to own my very own shotgun. From age ten, I had an air gun and hunted the woods and fields around my home for small birds, rats and rabbits, and in fact, for anything that moved. I had books on wildlife and my eldest brother used to get the Shooting Times and lots of American magazines dealing with hunting, shooting and fishing. So at a comparatively young age, I knew all about sporting guns of every kind and their uses. I also had, by the time I was twelve, a comprehensive knowledge of all kinds of ammunition.

My dream was building in intensity to the point that I spent any spare time I had in Waterford peering into the gun displays in the various hardware shops.

I should tell you now that when my family lived in Woodstown – 1928 to 1942 – the house had neither water nor electricity. We were 8 miles from town, two nearby "shops" sold only sweets and soft drinks, and after sunset, our recreation consisted of playing music, listening to a battery radio, reading and studying all kinds of catalogues, which we sent for by post. My favourites were Gun catalogues, which came from England and America.

At this time, a farmhand's wage was about ten shillings a week, a secretary/typist in an office was earning about one pound, and a city man was lucky if he earned three pounds a week. In this context, a double-barrelled shotgun cost at least six pounds, and most importantly, a licence for a shotgun cost two pounds a year, and finally a box of twenty-five cartridges cost four shillings for the cheapest brand. My pocket money was two shillings weekly, which made me much better off than my peers, but at thirteen, the sum total of my life's savings was about one pound.

Imagine my feelings then when I saw in John Hearn's Window in town, a single-barrelled shotgun priced at two pounds and ten shillings. It was a Harrington & Richardson's American-made farmers gun, designed for shooting vermin on the farm. I looked at it lovingly and that night I dreamt about it. All that week I could think of nothing else, and come Saturday, I went to the shop and asked if I could put a one pound deposit on the gun, the balance to be paid over the next year.

The man in the shop laughed at me, and then he saw my face, and his expression softened. "Well boy" he said, "if it means that much to you, I'll take your deposit." I thought my heart would burst with joy when he took the gun out of the window and placed it before me while he took my money and wrote a label which said "Sold to G. Cronin – Deposit paid one pound – balance due one pound ten shillings".

"You can put it back in the window now" he said, and come in now and again to keep it cleaned and oiled – it's yours now!"

As I picked it up and went towards the back of the window, I put it up to my shoulder and cocked the hammer, and could see rabbits rolling over dead from my single shot, and huge cock pheasants dropping from the sky in a cloud of feathers and pigeons and snipe and teal and mallard – all falling to what would be my unerring aim.

Of course I would have to be fifteen to get a licence, costing two pounds, and the cold reality was that I was only thirteen, but still, I was now the owner of that Harrington & Richardson single-barrel. Nevertheless, when you're thirteen, two years is a long, long time.

Time dragged by but at the end of that first year I had paid off the balance due on the gun, and went in to the shop every so often to clean and oil my treasured possession. Then I got a windfall – my father asked me if I would help out behind the counter in our bakery shop on Saturdays, and I jumped at the chance of making some extra money. I got five shillings a week in this way, and on my birthday I asked for cash in lieu of gifts from all and sundry. The result of all my financial manoeuvring was that by the middle of year two, I had saved almost seven pounds, enough for the gun licence and cartridges and plenty to spare.

One day I was on my way into the Hardware shop when I noticed, standing beside "my gun", a beautiful double-barrelled hammerless "French 75", and I was swamped by greed and ambition. Caution thrown to the wind, I almost ran into the shop to ask the price, not even hoping it would be within my range.

The man took the gun out of the window and handed it to me. I was lost in admiration of this wondrous thing, when he said, "if you like I'll take the Harrington in part exchange and the balance would be four pounds ten shillings."

My heart nearly stopped and I heard myself saying "It's a deal, and I'll bring the money tomorrow," which I did.

When I went home I told my mother the whole story, and she laughed and said "You're a great lad, and for your enterprise, I'll stand you half the licence fee." This meant that if only I was fifteen, I could fulfill my life's ambition – today!! But this was June and my fifteenth birthday wasn't until the end of September. There was nothing for it but to bide my time.

But then I heard one of the locals say that the Sergeant, who knew me well, was taking two weeks holidays on the first of July – the date the gun licence fell due!

On the second of July, I cycled the three miles to Passage East, where the Garda Station was. I filled out the licence application stating "Age: Fifteen years". Being tall for my age and being unknown to the guard on duty, I had decided to take the chance, and having paid the two pounds fee, I got on my bike and departed post haste. It would take a week to issue the licence, they said.

The next week seemed like a year, and on the Friday, the duty guard cycled into the yard and I fled, not knowing whether he was bringing the licence or a summons for misrepresentation. I watched the guard from hiding as he cycled out the gate and my mother called me from the house.

"There's something here for you," she said, waving a pink piece of paper. It was the licence!!

I cycled to town the next day and called to the shop where the man took my gun apart and wrapped it in that black paper, which was common in hardware shops. I bought a box of No. 4 cartridges and set off home with my precious cargo.

When I got out the road about two miles, I could wait no longer, and I stopped at the Island Lane, where a small inlet came from the River Suir. I unpacked the gun, assembled it, put two cartridges in the breech, slung the gun under my arm and walked down the bank of the inlet feeling like Lord Leitrim on the opening day of the grouse season. I imagined I would see a fine mallard rising from the mud, or at least a teal or a snipe. In reality it was a seagull which rose up from the inlet in front of me as I fired on him. The range was close, and I cut the poor bird in half with the attending cloud of feathers.

I didn't wait to pick him up, but cycled off as fast as I could until my heart had stopped hammering. I still felt like Lord Leitrim and I never forgot the thrill to this day nearly seventy years later.

Describing a bow-legged girl:
"She Wouldn't stop a Bonamh in a Boreen!"

The Shop

1938

My father, Richard (Dick) Cronin, born in 1881 at 12 John Street Waterford, set up business at that address under the style and title of ***Cronin's Bakery***. His father Owen Cronin, born in 1846, had bought the premises in about 1875 and had carried on business there selling bread, hardware, flour and meal, and trading in grain on the world market. In fact, he was importing wheat from Canada, among other countries, when the Canadian Pacific railway was being built.

Having gone to Limerick at age 16, my father served an apprenticeship of seven years with the Waterford & Limerick Railway, and became a qualified fitter. (My son Frank has the original indenture papers). He later worked for Dublin Port & Docks Authority as a fitter/engineer, and saw the introduction of the first turbines in Dublin Port. In 1904 he joined the British Royal Navy as an ERA – Engine Room Artificer, and served on Destroyers, Cruisers and Battleships, including a term in the China Seas.

I still remember the names of two of the ships he served on. One was "The Barfleur", a First-class battleship, and another was "The Vengence", a Canopus class battleship, which had twelve-inch guns with a range of approximately twenty miles.

Richard Cronin
Circa 1905

HMS Vengeance
In Hong Kong Circa 1905

In 1912 he came out of the Navy and returned home to Waterford to work the business with his father.

In the interim, Owen Cronin had bought a grist mill in Kilmacow, Co. Kilkenny, about two miles from Waterford City, and subsequently acquired a neighbouring property of some 37 acres on which stood a gate lodge, a school, and a fine old residence occupied by (I think) the Presentation Nuns, who ran the school. This property included "the pond" which formed the headrace for the mill, which could run for a day and a night on the full of the pond.

Over the next few years they set up a modern bakery at Kilmacow, a thriving milling business grinding oats, wheat, barley and maize for sale to the local farmers and to supply the shop in Waterford.

*Millstone from Cronin's Mills
Kilmacow, Co. Kilkenny
– Now demolished.*

My father used his engineering expertise to set up an electricity generating system for the mill and bakery, and also built the new bakery there. He subsequently modernized the shop in John Street, built a new bakehouse there of some 2,400 sq. feet, and installed a pair of Thompson Steam-Tube drawplate ovens in it, together with a power driven Dough Mixer and Dough Divider. All the machinery was powered by a Crossley gas engine, for which a new engine room was built, and a gas producer, run on coal and coke was installed to feed the Crossley. Finally, as there was no public electricity in existence, a dynamo was hooked up to the Crossley and electric power and light was produced for the house and the shop. At a time when public lighting was by gaslights, which was fairly dim, the shop stood out like a jewel in John Street.

The business of the mill and two bakeries had been booming and in 1920, prior to the big modernisation programme at John Street, my father had married Claire Spencer and they began living over the shop – my grandfather having retired to live in the house at the mill in Kilmacow.

However, just at the point where my father had launched the new business, disaster struck. There was a country-wide strike by Agricultural Labourers, and all my father's employees went out on strike in sympathy with them, even though he had no dispute with them. In fact, they were the best paid workers in the city. The net result was that the two bakeries and the mill had to close down and even our grain store in Conduit Lane off the quays, was picketed. There were forty men on the payroll at that time.

A cargo of oats had been purchased just before the strike and was stored, loose in Conduit Lane on four floors of the building, and my mother, who was pregnant at the time, had to help out at the store by turning the oats with a miller's shovel to prevent the grain from overheating and going bad, and hopefully saving the cargo.

I was born in September of that year, 1923, and the men had stayed out for eleven months, which resulted in a huge bank overdraft for my father, as he had lost heavily during the strike.

In the twelfth month, a deputation arrived at the door of the shop at midnight, with the proposal that "the lads would be satisfied to come back to work on the following Monday" even though the agricultural labourers were still on strike.

Needless to say by that time the whole injustice of the thing had stuck "crosswise" in my father's gullet, and he replied in caustic terms, comparing them to "a pack of cowardly cur dogs come back to lick up their vomit." "Well," he said, "it was swept out 12 months ago!" He never employed one of them again, or even any of their relatives.

By the end of the strike the modernisation programme, which was to have been a huge success, ended up – not just for that reason – as a struggle to overtake the losses which had been incurred during the strike. But my father *did* overtake those losses, chiefly by concentrating on the trade in flour and grain, and he showed an uncanny instinct in watching the grain market and taking some huge gambles on the movement of international prices. In short, he brought the business back into profit over the next seven or eight years, and ended up – by repute – one of the richest men in the city.

As part of the recovery plan, my father established a poultry farm at the mill in Kilmacow, and to do this, he purchased the winners of the world's laying competitions held in England, and also the prize-winning hens of various breeds of fowl all over Britain. The breeds he bought were Buff Rocks, White Wyandottes, Barred Rocks, Rhode Island Reds, Jersey Giants, White and Black Leghorns, and the produce, eggs, were being exported at good prices to England.

Then in the 1930s, the Irish government, led by deValera, embarked on the "Economic War". All the ports were closed to imports and exports, and anything which had to be imported was subject to prohibitive tariffs and excise duty. Up to then, Waterford was exporting huge numbers of livestock, cattle, sheep and pigs, and we had the largest bacon factory in Europe, namely Denny's. In fact, most of the employment in the city was provided in the docks. The shipping industry, in all its aspects, was the lifeblood of the city which was known as "Waterford of The Ships".

As far as the Cronin business was concerned, the effect was disastrous. There was no more export of eggs, the price of which fell from one shilling and sixpence a dozen, to fourpence a dozen, which was absolutely uneconomic, and I recall that three hundred pure-bred champion fowl were sold to a poulterer for seventeen pounds – a mere fraction of their value.

Flour, maize and all grain could no longer be imported, and the grain store had to close down. The mill also ceased to function and in fact, all mills had to be licensed and be given a quota saying how much you would be allowed to grind. Our capacity at Kilmacow as 200 tons per week, but when our license came, the quota was two and a half tons per week. At that point, my grandfather closed the mill. The bakery there had already closed following the strike.

The effect of the economic war on the national economy was devastating. The farmers suffered immeasurably due to lack of markets. For instance, they were told by politicians to "throw the calves in the ditch", and I vividly remember seeing two calves being sold outside our shop for one shilling and sixpence, and a three year old bullock being sold in the street for thirty shillings. Milk was being poured down the drains – literally – and the object of the whole exercise was "to starve John Bull", cutting off all our own lifelines in the process, and it lasted long enough to shrink the Cronin business to near extinction.

During this period, my grandfather died, the mill was sold (for buttons) to appease the bank and "the Convent" and its lands were also sold, leaving only the shop and a shrinking trade in bread.

Next came the Government order controlling the price of bread, a vote-catching ploy. The price of flour and other ingredients was not controlled, nor were wages, fuel etc. Our staff shrank to four or five, and the writing was on the wall.

The family home had been in Woodstown from 1928 to 1942, and about 1936 my father was taken ill with mastoid trouble in both ears, and spent almost 12 months in hospital in Dublin. During that time, my mother cycled into Waterford very early each morning – 8 miles – and ran the business, cycling home to Woodstown each night. My father had ten operations on his ears and throat, and seven of those were done by Oliver St. John Gogarty, and three were done by Dr. Curtin, a surgeon at the Eye and Ear Hospital in Adelaide Road, Dublin. Gogarty was a high-flying social figure at the time, and had his own private aeroplane and his own nursing home in Baggot Street, and he charged the earth for his services. My father paid him £300 for one operation, which was not successful and ended up having the job successfully done by Dr. Curtin, whose fee was £30!

Anyway, the final chapters concerning the shop in John Street are detailed elsewhere in this saga, but to give you some idea of the scale of operations, I shall enumerate the staff, which consisted of the following:-

- Three shop assistants cum bookkeepers
- Three van men
- Three porters cum cleaners and delivery
- Thirteen bakers
- One engine attendant and
- Three housemaids, who lived in.

The balance of forty was employed in the mill and the grain store on the docks.

I should mention also that our bread was famous for quality and our Christmas Bracks were known worldwide. I can remember tea-chests being filled with bracks and shipped to Australia and America. When the bakery was in full swing, we were using a hundred sacks of flour per

Cronin's Bakery sold the following lines:-

Fancy Bread	
Viennas (Ducks)	3d
Coburgs (Cobs)	3d
Batons	3d

Batch Bread	
Buns	2 ½d
Turnovers aka Carrick Grinders	2 ½d
Ballyduffs	2 ½d

Bracks
5/-
4/-
3/-
2/-
1/-
6d

Loaves	
Small	2 ½ d
Large	4 ½ d

Pans	
Large	5d
Small	3d
Ring	5d
Basket	5d

Brown Rounds	6d
Soda Rounds	6d
Sultana Rounds	8d
Bread Rolls	2d
Fasting buns	1d

week, which was two hundred ten-stone bags and at the end this was down to two and a half sacks per week.

During the war – which was known as "the emergency" – the law was such that no white flour could be milled or used to make bread. The order of the day was brown flour and brown bread – known as "Black Bread". This regime went on from 1939 to 1947, and the law was rigidly enforced, any contravention being met by heavy fines or imprisonment.

Things, however, had become desperate, and we (my father and I) decided to enter the black market in white flour

The weights were avoirdupois:-

16 ounces	=	1 pound	=	1 lb.
14 pounds	=	1 stone	=	1 st.
8 stone	=	1 hundredweight	=	1 cwt.
10 stone	=	1 bag (of flour).		
20 stone	=	1 sack (of flour).		

The money we used was as follows (pre-decimal):-

4 farthings	1 penny	1d
2 halfpennies	1 penny	1d
12 pence	1 shilling	1/- (1s)
20 shillings	1 pound	£1

Coins	Notes
¼ d	10/- (10s)
½ d	£1
1d	£5
3d	£10
6d	£20
1/- (1s)	£50
2/- (2s)	
2/6 (2s 6d)	

to try to save the business. My father's expertise in the milling business came into play here, and through various contacts, a length of milling silk was obtained and he and I went to work each night after the shop closed, and worked until 2 a.m. sifting the regulation brown flour into its components, i.e. white flour, bran and pollard, and everything had to be cleaned up and hidden before the bakehouse staff came on duty at 4 a.m. The white flour could then be sold for one pound per stone – the brown flour cost approximately three shillings and six pence per stone, and a very small amount of white bread was baked twice a week to cater for invalids and such like.

Richard Cronin
Circa 1922

The drill was that I would get up first in the mornings and open the shop and start the day's work, get the one van loaded and deal with the early morning trade. My father would stay in bed until about eleven and then appear in the shop.

Now my father was a short man, only 5 ft 4½ ins. tall, but he was fifteen stone in weight – 46 ins. in the chest and 48 ins plus in the waist – and after a late night was often too tired for formality. He just kicked off his shoes, loosened his tie, and dropped his pants where he stood, and fell into bed practically fully clothed, minus shoes and pants.

On one particular occasion, when I opened the shop in the morning, a Jewish businessman from Dublin arrived and quietly asked me for eight stone of white flour in eight separate bags. I took out a ten-stone bag from hiding, and weighed out the eight bags onto the counter, stowing the remainder under the counter. I then took the money and proceeded to close up the eight bags which the client was taking out to his car. Our most trusted employee, Jimmy, was standing by keeping an eye out on the street for anyone who looked like a government inspector.

Just as I was closing bag number eight, Jimmy whistled from the street, and in walked a man unmistakably an inspector.

"I want to see the proprietor!" he said, in a peremptory tone.

"Just one moment, sir" I said, as I handed bag number eight to the customer, who departed swiftly.

"Jimmy," I called, "This man wants to see the boss. Would you run upstairs and call him please?"

Jimmy knew exactly what was going on, and he duly went upstairs and woke my father with the announcement that there was an inspector downstairs in the shop.

As described by Jimmy afterwards, "The man leapt out of bed, jumped into his trousers, shouldered his braces, and stepped into his shoes while donning his jacket, glasses and hat." Thus composed, he arrived into the shop, every inch the proprietor, and invited the inspector, who incidentally had declared himself, to accompany him into the office. Meanwhile, I told Jimmy to take the half sack of white flour to the shop next door, and say he'd collect it later.

The inspector had been seated in the office with my father standing over him. The man seemed to go quite pale, and got up to leave, with my father following him. I didn't hear what had been said earlier, but as he got to the door, my father took him gently by the arm, and nose to nose, said quietly "I wouldn't come back here if I were you – it would be very VERY unhealthy, and another thing, *Mister*, this country will never be right until people like you are strung up by the arse and shot like a dog in the street." The man walked away, very quickly, and he never came back.

My father stood at the counter, his face flushed with a dying anger and I saw him struggling to get his hand into his trousers pocket, unsuccessfully, and no wonder, for he had his trousers on back to front! Jimmy saw his predicament and guffawed, and then I saw it and I laughed out loud, and then my father, standing on his dignity up to then, spotted the problem and groaned "Oh Bloody Wars" before exploding into laughter.

So ended a very funny episode, which I recall with great affection for my father.

❧

Owen Cronin – My Paternal Grandfather

Owen Cronin was born in 1846, the year of the great famine, and I believe he came from Fermoy, Co. Cork. He died when I was quite young and in all of my memory of him, he lived in the mill house at Kilmacow, Co. Kilkenny.

Because of this, I saw him rarely, except for Sunday visits to the mill during which he and my father had long discussions about the price of grain, on world markets, and the business of the mill.

I remember him as a quiet old man, bald, with piercing blue eyes and a walrus moustache. He fascinated me, as a child, and I remember that he had a

Owen Cronin – Circa 1890

walking stick with a devil's face on the knob, which frightened me. My only real contact with him was on the occasions when he used to complain to my mother about my escapades in the mill – and they were many! Most memorable was when I decapitated his prize rooster by throwing a slate at it. His exact words were "That one is a little devil". Sunday visits to the mill were suspended for three Sundays after that.

My grandfather knew all about horses and horses were his hobby all his life. He was regarded as "a great judge of a horse". In his young days, he was friendly with a horse dealer named Anderson, who used to buy horses (troopers) for the British Army – and for Charles Bianconi, father of the stage-coach network, which served as public transport at that time. At a later stage Owen Cronin became a friend of the famous Bianconi, and used to buy horses directly for him.

As a young man, he was sent to Leeds, in England, to learn the textile trade. When he returned, he toured the country selling boots, to the mostly barefoot country people.

In or about 1875 he bought the premises at No. 12 John Street from a Mr. Murphy. He then set up shop in grain, feedstuff and hardware. Then, because there was a bakehouse attached to the premises, he also set up in the bread business. In time, this became his main trade. Later, he acquired the mill and the Hermitage at Kilmacow.

When my father was married, Owen Cronin gave him the property at John Street, plus a sizeable amount of cash – £10,000, I believe.

Once, I came upon him at his bureau in the mill house, when he was having a raw egg and a glass of whiskey. I was about four years old at the time and asked him for a drink out of his glass. He gave the glass to me, with one of his rare smiles, and I took a goodly slug! I thought I had swallowed a red-hot poker, as I coughed and gasped for breath.

He patted my back and sad to me; "Now boy. What you just had was *Drink*. So, always remember this… It's a good servant but a damn bad master!" I never forgot those words.

Owen Cronin was never known to say a bad word about anyone. He was most highly respected in business circles and was noted for his integrity. I just wish I had known him better.

James the Landlord

1939

When I lived in Woodstown in the 1930s our house was on the edge of a sandy beach which stretched for half a mile in either direction and our landlord, James, lived in the cottage next door.

James was a lean, old, guy in his late eighties. He had a full head of curly hair, a square foxy beard and spent a lot of his days chopping firewood from a huge stock of logs in his front yard. In his young days James had been a stone mason and his wife had been the cook in the "big house" which now stood deserted on the wooded estate nearby.

There was an eight foot high storm wall which ran the length of our house – and the cottage next door. This protected both properties from the sea when the tides ran high. In the winter we had to barricade the french windows at the back of the house and I clearly remember going to sleep to

James the Landlord, collecting cockles

the regular thump of waves crashing against that wall. In the summer holidays those french windows were always open and we could just walk out, pop over the wall and be on the beach, or in the sea if the tide was a high one.

On a fine evening, after she had listened to the nine o'clock news on our battery radio, my mother would stroll out to the storm wall for a quiet smoke and a chat with James. He would also have heard the news and it would be discussed in detail, as well as the weather forecast. James knew how to turn on the radio and how to connect the batteries but he had no clear idea of how it worked or what "airwaves" were. The Irish broadcasting station was "Athlone", the BBC was just "The English Station" and the whole apparatus was popularly known as "The Wireless".

On one occasion James's wireless broke down and when the local bus arrived he handed it to the bus driver with instructions to bring it to the wireless man in town and ask him how much to fix it. On his return the bus driver reported that it would cost thirty shillings to fix it – it needed a new valve. James was shocked at the cost and told the bus driver to enquire "what would he charge just to fix Athlone!"! After much argy-bargy he capitulated, paid the thirty bob and the wireless was returned "as good as new!"

I recall the time when King George V of England was ill and dying and there were hourly bulletins from Buckingham Palace regarding his condition. Mother and James were in conversation about it:

Front view of our home at Woodstown early 1930s.
NB. The slats across the lower part of the window were to keep the local goats, which belonged to James the Landlord, from parking on the lower window sill.

"Well James," she said. "What do you think about the news?"

"Ah ma'am they're bulletin about it all day," he replied, "and I think meself that the poor bloody bugger is shagged."

He was right you know and the king died next day.

When the war came and the German propaganda machine came into play the infamous James Joyce, or Lord Haw Haw as he was known, could be heard coming through the BBC line and contradicting everything the English announcer would say. Because of the varying strength of the signals, each station would come and go amid bursts of crackling interference. James thought their contests were very entertaining and he would refer to the announcers as *The German* and *The Englishman*.

One evening the contest had been hot & heavy and James described it to my mother as follows:

"*The Englishman* came on the wire and he commenced giving out the news and the next thing was *The German* got up behind him and shoved him off the wire. Then, after a while, *The Englishman* got strong and managed to get back up on the wire and you couldn't hear *The German* at all, except in fits and starts. But then, after *The German* got a rest, he got up on the wire along with *The Englishman* and they started shouting at each other and there was a fierce struggle and be the 'tarnal didn't *The Englishman* get the better of *The German* and pushed him off altogether. Then *The German* got right wicked and commenced shovellin' gravel up agin the wire for pure spite. After that we got the rest of the English news and there was no sign of Lord Haw Haw, but begod it was a right battle between the two of 'em."

Incidentally, the "gravel" was radio interference which occurred when the station was being "jammed" and there was a conflict of signals.

James told my mother on another occasion that he was giving up listening to the weather forecast from Athlone and was changing his allegiance to *The Englishman* because he was "giving out much better weather!"

At an earlier stage I began getting slightly envious of James because he owned three goats which provided him with milk. He also had two dogs, Mikey and Barney, who used to come running when I played the mouth organ and they would sit down in front of me and howl unmercifully.

I had a dog of my own, a female named Jack, which I had acquired from a man called Larry who was famous for having a wooden leg. Incidentally, for a fee of a penny Larry would hand you his stick and let you hit his leg with it. This went on for some time until one kid hit him an unmerciful whack on the wrong leg! Needless to say, the air turned blue on that occasion and the culprit's parentage was called into question in no uncertain manner and this ended the "penny a whack" game.

Now, I couldn't wait to have my own goat and I got a kid through the generosity of a pal I used to meet on the school bus. He told me to call to his parents' farm and I could take one of the kid goats recently born there. I gladly

accepted and having walked the two miles to his place I
then had to carry the kid back to my home in my arms.
There is an old saying *"Even a hen is heavy if you carry it
far enough!"* – and I really learned the truth of that by the
time I got home.

With the aid of a baby's bottle I fed the kid until it was
strong enough to join James's "herd" as they went out to
graze. I called her Dora and she would follow me about like a
dog. When in time she had kids herself and was giving milk
I only had to whistle and she would come to be milked.

But to return to James – he was an expert carpenter,
though that was not his trade. He was also a great gardener
and a mine of information on all kinds of plants and vegetables. He had a large garden which supplied him with

*Woodstown 1937 - Left to Right James (The Landlord), Two work-
ers at the Barron Estate, Billy Gough - worker at the Salmon Weir
next door to our home.*

vegetables all year round and he tilled it himself until he was in his late ninety's. As a boy, I hung around him a lot and he would help me with small carpentry jobs and advise me how to handle and feed my ferret, show me how to dig lugworms for fishing, how to milk a goat, or to harvest a can of cockles on a Friday to be eaten in lieu of fish. In short, he was the source of information about anything except new fangled contraptions like the wireless!

One day I found him in the garden, sitting on an old worn bench in a sunny corner and he was chewing on an onion. I was amazed and asked him why a raw onion? He said "you should eat everything that grows and comes in season – that's why the lord put it there."

James' brother Patsy lived with him and he seemed very odd to me. It was said that he was a bit daft, to put it mildly. Apparently he had at one time farmed a smallholding in Rosduff, a nearby townsland, and he had kept pigs.

An apochryphal story told against Patsy related how when pig-feed went up in price he decided that, since pigs had no intelligence, he would simply reduce the rations to the irreducible minimum and maybe even train them to do without food altogether. The story goes that he almost had them trained when for some strange reason they died!

Our house on Woodstown Beach was a double-fronted villa type building, standing in its own grounds, and the rent was thirty pounds a year. On one occasion, when my father was paying the rent, James asked him if he would consider buying the property. The asking price was three hundred pounds and my father thought that this was exorbitant and didn't buy. Such were the economies of the 1930s! Today's value on the same house would be a hundred and fifty thousand, at a conservative estimate.

Well, we lived there until 1942 when we returned to the city to live over the shop at 12 John's Street. I donated Dora the goat to James for the enhancement of his "herd" and I believe she lived a long and happy life there. James lived to be over a hundred and was still chopping his own firewood until a few days before his death.

My childhood in Woodstown was nothing short of idyllic and I have many happy memories of my time there. One thing I will never forget is the thrill of stepping out the french windows, over the wall and onto the beach in the early morning, when it had been swept clean by the tide, and running along with sheer exuberance knowing that mine were the only footprints on the beach.

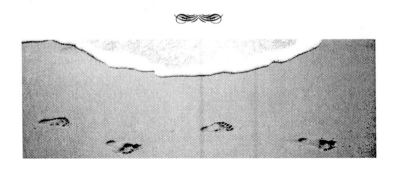

The Snipe Shoot

1939

Jim Skids was one of the "characters" of his village. He was of indeterminate age, wore a flat cap, a threadbare gabardine coat and hob-nailed boots. He was professionally unemployed, by which I mean that he was never known to willingly do a day's work. He was a known poacher, of trout, salmon and any kind of game you care to mention. An expert with dogs and ferrets he knew every rabbit-run, every pheasant roost in the parish and if put to the test could probably tell you exactly the whereabouts of the local gamekeeper at any time of the day. In consequence of all this knowledge he had quite a reputation as a guide and ghillie and part of his scant income came from taking shooting parties out for a day's sport on the bogs and stubble fields in the area.

Skids was quite old when I knew him and I reckoned he was well into his sixties, because his sight was beginning to fail. His pride and joy was on a Monday evening to sit behind a pint of stout in his local and name drop about the people he had out for the shoot on the Sunday – an the fabulous bag of game that they shot – thanks to his "expert guidance". Incidentally, nobody could tell why he was called "Skids" – he just was!

He had an ancient double-barrelled shotgun with hammer action and Damascus twisted steel barrels, with patterns inlaid in gold on the box of the gun. It was a real beauty of a gun and had been a gift from a grateful client many years ago.

Skids was never known to buy cartridges yet he generally seemed to have a few in his pocket. His technique for

A shooting party at woodstown 1938.
Left to Right Harry Tobin, Geoffrey Spencer (my 1st Cousin),
Self with new shotgun. Dick Cronin (my brother)

acquiring them was unique. When he took a party out to shoot they would foregather at the edge of a bog, where they would expect to meet Snipe, and maybe the odd Teal or Mallard, and Skids would arrange the guns in a certain order before they set out to walk the bog. Before the start, however, he would approach some guy in the line and hold out a few cartridges in his hand. "Would you ever swap these number fours for number eights, 'cos I only have fours and we'll be meetin' snipe?" The client would invariably toss him five or six and would magnanimously tell him to keep his own few cartridges. He never seemed to have the right sized shot and by using this ploy he managed to end up with a pocketful of all sizes.

One particular day I was a member of a party which had engaged Skids as a Ghillie for a day's bog shoot and as we progressed across the first bog snipe were rising in front of us and were falling here and there. Then I saw Skids taking a shot back, behind the line of guns. I could see no snipe although he went over and picked up a bird.

"I didn't see that snipe getting up Jim" I said.

"'Twould be hard for ye to see him boy" he answered, "I shot that one on the ground!"

It was the most outrageous fib I had ever heard and what had actually happened was that the spaniel had missed that particular snipe, which another member of the party had shot, and Skids had taken the ball "on the hop" so to speak. It was then that I realised that his sight was failing and that he could no longer see the little snipe rising.

I said nothing, for I couldn't see him lose face by having nothing to show at the end of the day. Anyway, he would normally defer to his "guests" when birds were scarce.

That was the last time I shot with this marvellous old poacher, though I heard that he carried on being "The Ghillie" for another year or so. Even after he was dead & gone shooting men gathering in the local after a day out could be heard quoting some of Skids' tall tales. If I had to write his epitaph it would read;-

Jim Skids
He was a character.
R.I.P.

> ### *Giving a girl "the eye" –*
> *"He was lookin' at her like a hen lookin' into a bottle"*

Work on a Timber Gang

1942

In September 1942 I had just left school and had decided I was going into the National Forestry Service. I made an application and found that I would not be admitted to the forestry college at Avondale, Co. Wicklow, unless (a) I was a farmer's son, or (b) I had experience in forestry. I could not meet either of these criteria, and so I decided to join a timber gang and gain the necessary experience.

The war was at its height and at the time timber was at a premium both for firewood and for commercial purposes. Consequently there was a lot of activity on farms and estates, which had saleable timber and so there were many timber gangs active in my area.

There was a big old estate originally owned by Lord Bessborough – one of the Ponsonby family, which had been bought by the Oblate Fathers. The mansion had been converted into a Seminary, and they were selling off the timber to recoup their original outlay.

The estate was in the village of Piltown, Co. Kilkenny, twelve miles from Waterford where I lived, and two and half miles from Carrick on Suir. This village had a Creamery, a hardware shop, a pub, a grocery shop, an undertaker, and a population of about forty or fifty people.

There were two gangs of timber men working the estate, one gang was felling the hardwood, mainly huge oak trees which dotted the parkland, and which were going for firewood to fuel the steam boiler at the Creamery, and the other one was felling the softwood, Spruce and Scotch Fir, which went to a sawmill in Waterford. The man who

The Timber gang – Mikey, Jack, Dan and Petey

ran the softwood gang was a friend of my family and he agreed to let me join his team for the experience.

So it was when my mother and I went to Piltown one Saturday seeking a place for me to stay five days a week. We found a vacancy with a Kerry woman, Essie Brosnan by name. The digs would cost four shillings per day, sharing a room with an assistant from the local shop, and I could get a bus to go home at the week-end. All was agreed and the following Monday morning I reported for work, carrying my own axe, with a certain amount of self-assurance. I had been working on a farm in Woodstown during the summer, and I felt very fit and tough enough for anything the timber scene could throw at me.

The gang consisted four men, Mikey, the foreman, Danny, his right hand man, and two car-men, Peter and Jack, whose job it was to pull out the timber after it was felled,

Carman Petey Welsh and helper
at Bessborough Estate Winter 1942.

and cut it into lengths of twelve, fourteen and sixteen feet, and cart it a mile and a half to the railhead at Fiddown. They were paid by the ton. I remember particularly the wonderful smell of resin from freshly cut Spruce, mixed with the smell of leaves on the ground and the faint smell of the camp fire where the men were having their lunch break. It was mid-day when I cycled into the camp on that first day and was welcomed by Mikey the foreman,

"Will ye have the tay?" he asked. I declined, having had a snack in the digs when I checked in there earlier.

"Show me the little hatchet you have," he said smiling indulgently. I did so and he examined it "That's not a bad edge ye have," he said. The others examined it and there seemed to be a general air of amusement. I had no idea why this was, but it got my hackles up slightly.

Yours truly
On the Timber Gang

"Here" said Mikey, now engrossed in filling his pipe, "While I'm having a smoke, maybe you'd take the front out of that tree there," indicating a black Spruce, about three feet in diameter.

I took off my jacket, spat on my hands and squared

up to my task, determined to show these guys a thing or two. My first two strokes took out a piece of wood about two inches wide, and half an inch deep, and the shock to my arms and wrists was unbelievable. A quiet snigger from Danny and the Car men reached my ears as I went in again with no better results.

Mikey let me go on for ten minutes, by which time the Car men had left to get their horses, and then he said "Here boy, take a rest for yourself and let me give you a hand." I did so, and watched this little man – he was five foot four inches and in his late fifties – as he picked up an axe with a seven pound head, and addressed the job – my "axe" had a three and a half pound head.

This was a Specimen Scots Fir Tree - 78 feet to the first fork - Which Mikey Wall (on Right) and I felled at the Grand Gates of the Bessborough Estate in Piltown, Co. Kilkenny in 1942.

Well, as he hacked into that tree, chips four and five inches wide, and two inches deep began to fly and in ten minutes flat, it was ready for the saw.

"Come on now," he said, "get on the other end of the saw" – it was a five and a half foot cross-cut saw, and I knew how to use it so I knelt down and Mikey passed one end of the saw to me and we began to cut until we were about a third of the way into the tree.

"Now boy, get a hammer and two wedges out of the bag there, and knock the wedges into the cut to keep the weight off the saw."

I picked up the seven-pound sledge hammer, and did the needful. We continued sawing and when we got two inches or so from the breast cut, I uncoupled my handle and he withdrew the saw from the far side.

"Now" he said, "stay close to the butt and watch the top of the tree." He took the hammer and drove the wedges in until the tree went out of the perpendicular, and down she came with a crunching thump. I sat down on the stump, and

Carman Petey Welsh

Mikey filled his pipe, and when I tried to get up, I found I was stuck! Mikey laughed – the resin had flowed up in the stump, and I had to yank myself free.

"That'll only season the trousers for ye," he said.

In that first day, Mikey and I felled four big spruces, and I honestly thought the day would never end. When Mikey said, "We'll knock off now," the relief was immense.

"We'll hide the gear here 'til morning," he said. "Bring up the bag with the other two wedges."

I went to oblige but when I caught the neck of the sack, though the wedges in it weighed no more than three pounds, I just couldn't lift it off the ground. I was completely exhausted,

Left to right - Jack Roche and Petey Walsh (Carmen),
Larry Cantwell and Claus Cantwell, Mikey Wall (Foreman),
Danny Sullivan, G. Cronin, Dick Cronin..

and just about managed to walk the short distance to the spot where we had left our bikes.

Then I discovered that Mikey would cycle **seventeen miles** to where he lived near Clonmel and he would cycle the same distance back to work the next day! This little man was made of IRON!!

When I got back to the digs, I just ate my dinner and fell into bed and slept around the clock. The process of waking and getting up is something I shall never forget. Every muscle in my whole body was screaming in agony, and it took me quite a while to loosen up. Fortunately, I was left with Danny that day, trimming the trees we had cut the day before, and cutting them into lengths for the car men. This was a different exercise, equally strenuous but at least I was not on my knees punishing every muscle in my back.

Mikey had been off through the woods checking trees marked for felling, and deciding how they might be got to the nearest road or track for transport. After the lunch break he said, "Come on now young man. We'll go to the shop and get you a proper hatchet" – he never called it an axe – "That thing you have is only fit for making kindlin'." At the hardware shop I watched while he went through the rack of axes, and finally he handed me one. It was a "Black Prince" with a hickory handle and a five and a half pound head. "This should do ye nicely," he said, and as we took it to the counter I saw that the assistant was my room-mate at the digs. "That will be thirteen shillings," he said, and I paid up.

On our return to the camp Mikey showed me how to sharpen the axe with a file. Then he demonstrated how exactly to use it, left handed and right handed, how to cut the boots – big roots – off a tree prior to putting the saw to it, how to under-cut when starting the breast cut etc. In fact, the things expected of an efficient timber man. Then he left me on my own to practice as I trimmed the trees already felled and he departed with Danny to fell some more.

On the days that followed, I got to know the car men, and I marveled at their expertise in getting two and three-ton logs past all kinds of obstructions on the tracks where a cart could be used. I learned how to use levers, skids, stobs, squeezers, wire ropes, chains, combinations of block and tackle, shear legs and Weston Block for lifting logs onto a cart and tricks and dodges too numerous to mention. Nothing was impossible to these guys and no stick – their term for a sixteen foot log – was too big or awkward to be got onto a cart. Their horses too were expert in their own way and they knew the routine for each kind of procedure.

The whole experience amounted to what today would be termed a steep learning curve, and it stood me in good stead for the rest of my life. The work was physically very demanding in dry weather and even more so when movement was hampered with wet clothing, but very rewarding.

The lunch time breaks were great fun and very educational in more ways than one, and as time went on and my body became attuned to the work, I could sail through the day, go shooting duck after dinner, and later on, cycle into

Lunch break with my brother Dick

Carrick-on-Suir to the Forester's Hall and dance the night away to the strains of a band who knew only three tunes!

I stayed with that gang until the end of January, when I was being paid twenty-six shillings a week, and the friendships I made at that time lasted for many years. In the event, I never joined the Forestry Division, and instead went into my father's Bakery business, as he needed my help at the time. However, the knowledge and experience gained came in very useful later in my life. But that's another story.

The Digs In Dublin

1944

It was in the autumn of 1945 when I set out for Dublin where I was to work at *The Swiss Chalet* Bakery and learn the confectionery trade. I was to do a year's stint, without pay, and my father would pay for my board and lodgings – thirty shillings per week.

So it was that I arrived at teatime in the "digs" at Mespil Road by the canal in Dublin. It was an old Georgian house with ten granite steps leading up to the front door. The door was answered by Mary, the maid, a good-looking dark-haired girl with a complexion so pale it suggested prison pallor. I waited in that lofty hallway, which had a faint aroma of polish and boiled cabbage. Mary went to call the landlady.

Dublin landladies of that time – it was known as "the emergency" here, or "the war", in other countries – had the reputation of being somewhat less than generous. In fact, it was jokingly said that you could tell a landlady sitting on the beach because she would pick up pebbles and squeeze them and drops of blood would come out. The truth was that they had a very difficult time catering for their guests, because all staple food was rationed – tea, butter, sugar etc. – and anything not rationed would be at black market prices.

Now the landlady emerged from the nether regions – she lived in the basement with a flock of cats, her husband Peter, and Mary the maid. Peter had the same prison pallor as Mary, and was tall and thin, so thin, in fact, he looked as if he had been ironed. I only saw him twice in the year I spent there. His wife, Mrs. Keller, on the other hand was the complete opposite. She was no more than five feet tall and weighed in at around eighteen stone. Her complexion was ruddy, her black hair was parted in the middle and disappeared down her back, and her fat face was adorned by a black moustache. An imposing figure, no doubt about it. She was a pleasant enough lady and my briefing was concise. Rent was thirty shillings weekly, payable every Tuesday; I got a key for the front door and could come and go as I pleased as long as I made no noise at night. Mary would show me to my room, and tea (the evening repast) would be in the dining room in fifteen minutes.

The bedroom was upstairs. It contained two beds, one large wardrobe, which could be locked, a tallboy with two drawers allocated to each inmate, a large window which overlooked the garden and also Iris Kellet's Equestrian School. The ceiling was lofty as befits a Georgian house, with an ornate centrepiece and the floor was covered with the coldest lino I ever experienced. The room was unheated!!

Having put my case under number two bed, I checked where the bathroom was – there was only one – and went down to the dining room. Nine men were seated at the table having their tea, and I was appointed to the tenth place with my own sugar bowl and butter dish. The ration, which arrived on Thursday, was half a pound of sugar and six ounces of butter. Mary, with something resembling a flourish, presented me with a plate bearing a rasher, egg and sausage, noted by all the company. I was to learn later that this was only an "introductory offer", and the standard tea was egg on toast. Breakfast was one boiled egg and toast, and lunch was the main meal. Supper consisted of one glass of milk – watery!

The personnel were a mixed bag consisting of one civil servant (Land Commission), one book-keeper (Johnston Mooney & O'Brien), one High Court clerk, one thirty-two year old chronic medical student, four divinity students (Protestant), one trainee radio officer, and myself, trainee confectioner.

The guests had the use of the drawing room, which had a piano but no fire after about nine o'clock in the evening. This was no big deal in the autumn, but as winter set in, it was a different story. Still it didn't affect me too much as I went out most nights to attend dance classes, which was my thing at that time, and because I had a bicycle!

Because of my bicycle, I got a key to the side door of the house, which gave access to the downstairs hallway where I could park my bike. The side door was situated under those imposing granite steps which led up to the front door but in addition it also gave access to the turf store, which filled the space beneath the front steps.

One night I came in about ten o'clock. There was a heavy frost and the house was freezing, so much so that the few guys in the dining room had been burning their evening papers to try and keep up the temperature. I, on the other hand, decided that enough was enough and taking the empty bucket, I went out the front door, down the steps and in the side door where I quietly filled the bucket with turf and made a triumphal re-entry to the dining room, where we soon had a roaring fire going. A second bucket was filled, and as more guys came in and shared the welcome heat, the atmosphere became positively convivial.

About midnight, the main topic was how we might continue our new found comfort, when one of the divinity students produced a large waterproof cape of the type supplied to the Local Defence Force. It was big enough to double as a ground sheet for camping out. This was carried out the front door and returned full of turf. This supply was stored on top of the large ornate cornice over the sideboard, two further cape loads were carried upstairs and stored in the wardrobe in my room – all the clothes having been removed and hung up all over the place. By one a.m. everything was secured and all concerned sworn to secrecy. We were all tired, but warm and happy.

Now there was a "houseboy" employed in the digs who did all the cleaning and polishing. He was a diminutive little fellow whose name was Willie, and he was "a couple of bricks short of a cartload", so to speak. However, he stopped me in the hall one lunchtime, saying –

"Tell me now, Mr. Cronin, you're an educated man who would know the answer to this puzzle. How is it that one bucket of turf can produce two buckets of ashes?"

I was taken aback and decided to blind Willie with science, and I answered "Well, Willie, it has to do with the inverse ratio between the height of the chimney and the shape and size of the bucket."

He went off muttering something about education and I guessed I had put him off the track, at least for the moment.

The following evening, however, all hell broke loose. Willie had had an accident and suffered a cut to his face and had been to the hospital for attention. Apparently Willie had succeeded in unlocking the door of the wardrobe in my room, and when a couple of hundredweight of turf fell out on top of him, he fell over and struck his face on the corner of the wardrobe.

An inquisition was to follow that night, and a rapid whip around the lads produced the story that collectively we had bought a couple of bags of turf to try to keep ourselves warm, and smuggled them into the digs, and we felt sure Mrs. Keller would not want any publicity about the sad plight of her guests.

My roommate and I made a big fuss about invasion of privacy in having our wardrobe broken into. Well, the store of turf was confiscated, but we still had the lot we had hidden over the sideboard in the dining room, and we did get an extra bucket of turf per night thereafter, also every man swore to be on his best behaviour in future.

There was, however, another dark plot being hatched. My roommate, who had a good job in the Four Courts, bought a small electric fire in a pawnshop down town and it came in a little attaché case with a comparatively stout lock. He reckoned, in any event, that Willie's career in lock picking had come to an end. Well, the luxury of being able to warm pyjamas with the little fire was almost unbearable. In fact, after a while we were having visitors from other rooms coming stealthily in for a warm, and there would often be six or seven "warmers" in the room at a time. Next there was the mystery of the escalating electricity bill, and operations had to be curtailed for a while until it was announced that the mystery couldn't be solved! Anyway, we survived the cold weather rather well, one way or another.

As with any male household where there is always a "wild card", we certainly had one in the person of Joey, the Radio Officer. On the day Joey got his remittance from home, he would pay for his digs and get well and truly drunk on whatever was left. He would roll in at midnight singing at the top of his voice, and be threatened with expulsion the next morning. During the week he made regular visits to the pawnshop, where his watch, his camera and everything else in sight would be pledged. On one particular night, we were warming ourselves at our private electric fire, when Joey arrived. He burst into our room singing, took off his shoes "not to be too noisy", and announced that we were to have a Céilí. He cavorted about the room doing his version of a "one handed reel" and in the process shed his jacket, his shirt, and then his trousers, all to great hilarity.

Suddenly, we heard Mrs. Keller's voice, as she puffed up the stairs and arrived on our landing, calling out "Mr. Tyler (Joey), is it you who's making all this noise?"

Joey, by this time down to his underwear, whipped off his shorts and rushed out onto the landing shouting "Coming my love!" The landlady disappeared down those stairs like a rabbit into a hole!!

❧

Joey did everyone a great service on another occasion. It was generally known that the medical student was "a toucher", i.e. he had borrowed money from all and sundry and had not repaid any of his debts. He was living well beyond his means and among other things, he went horse riding and had a very nice pair of riding boots for that purpose. Well, one Saturday when "the Medical" was out, Joey went around all the guests and took notes of what each person was owed. Then he disappeared and reappeared

125

just before teatime, and ceremoniously paid off all "the Medical's" debts.

Before we could ask for an explanation, "the Medical" burst into the room red as a turkey cock, shouting, "My room has been burgled and by good riding boots are missing."

Joey immediately took him by the arm and shepherded him to a chair. "Relax, man, and don't be getting so excited. Your boots are not missing at all, they're quite safe." "The Medical" was open-mouthed.

"Well, where are they?" he said belligerently.

"I'll give you the address," said Joey smiling indulgently as he fished a pawn ticket out of his pocket and handed it to "the Medical. "You can pick them up there any time you like."

There was a spontaneous cheer from the assembled gathering, and "the Medical" slunk out of the room, his face ashen by this time. A week later, he was gone from the digs, and meantime Joey was a hero, especially as he admitted he had made a small profit on the transaction.

❦

Another "event" which happened in the digs was when Mary, the maid, got a brainwave. She confided in me prior to making the suggestion to the landlady. The weekly ration of butter and sugar came on Thursdays and Mary was going to suggest that since "all the gentlemen were out of rations by Tuesday, the landlady should get the rations on Wednesday!"

On the same subject, I noticed that my butter ration began to diminish rapidly at one stage, and it was obvious that someone was helping himself in my absence. My problem was that I was out of the house first every morning, as I started work at eight o'clock, and everybody else went out about nine or later. This fact gave the thief ample opportunity to raid my butter dish.

At that time my elder brother, Dick, was working in a Chemist's shop on the other side of Dublin, and we met at odd weekends. I was telling him about my problem and he said –

"I'll give you some extract of malefern, which you can mix with some butter and leave it as bait for your thief."

When I asked what exactly this stuff was, he answered cheerfully "It's what they give to racehorses for constipation." I took it and baited my butter as instructed, and told only one person about the trap. My butter was never touched again! The person I told was my roommate. He left the digs soon afterwards. This ended my stay at the digs in Mespil Road.

❧

The next digs I found myself in, was at the top of Harcourt Street, and the rent was now two pounds a week. It was another Georgian house on the side of the street, and was run by a maiden lady in her fifties.

Miss Ruttle was an imperious lady with jet black hair (dyed), tall and large bosomed, and obviously wore a bulletproof corset which just about enabled her to get into the rather garish dresses she wore. She was militantly religious and just before we finished our evening meal, she would sweep into the dining room, preceded by her very pungent perfume, and order us all down on our knees to say the Rosary, followed by "the trimmings" which consisted of three Hail Marys for each of her special intentions, e.g. the souls in purgatory, propagation of the faith, girls who were keeping doubtful company (all named), etc. etc. etc. The trimmings took longer than the Rosary, and the whole performance was devoutly to be avoided. This we did, most of the time.

One night, it was someone's pay night and some of us went out for a drink – this was daring stuff – and returned about ten o'clock, to find "herself" straddling the welcome mat with arms folded.

"I've only one thing to say to you gentlemen," she said icily. "If you don't come home at a reasonable hour in future, you will ***not*** be allowed to join in the family Rosary."

One night, when Miss Ruttle announced that she was going out for the evening, four of us ventured into her drawing room, which was totally "off limits". The room was Victoriana personified, with hand painted cushions, a red plush chaise-longue, footstools, a sampler fire screen, bric-a-brac all over the place, and beautiful upright piano in an ebony case with matching stool. I promptly sat down at the piano, at which point the rest of the "guests" joined us, and in no time flat, we had a right royal sing song going.

We were in the middle of "You must have been a beautiful baby," when everything went suddenly quiet, and when I looked up from the keyboard – there she was, in the open doorway. I remember thinking of the scene in the sorcerer's apprentice when the wizard appears and stops the flood. The temperature in the room dropped to zero, and there followed a tirade of rhetoric that would have done credit to Hitler himself.

Well, we just about managed to maintain speaking terms – in a monosyllabic manner – for the remainder of my stay, which fortunately was only a few weeks, as my time in Dublin had run its course.

I made some friends in that place and in fact I still meet one of them for a drink every year since I came to live in Dublin permanently, nearly forty years ago.

On the timber gang when we'd be packing up in the evening, we could see flocks of crows (Rooks) making their way to the roosting place called "The Mountain Grove" ten or twelve miles away.
Mikey recalled a night when the weather was so bad that the crows had to walk to the mountain grove.

The Nuns At The Glue Pot

1946

It was five o'clock in the afternoon on the 16th of July 1946. The sky was dark and thunder rumbled intermittently. The rain came down like stair-rods and steam was rising from the warm road. I roused my three friends and we went downstairs for a drink before tea.

Being billeted over a pub wasn't such a bad idea on a day like this, especially in a seaside village. We were playing in a dance band in the local hall for the season – we were the dance-band – and we would start work about eight o'clock.

The pub was known locally as "The Glue Pot" and as the evening wore on and people ventured out after the rain and made their way towards the dance hall which would be packed with holiday makers. Right now, there were only two old fishermen sipping pints by the window, the barman, Pat, and the four of us at the back of the bar.

I was lifting a lager shandy to my lips when I heard voices and the door burst open and three men came in, all laughing uproariously. Two were fishermen and the third, called Ritchie, was obviously a returned exile. It turned out he was back from the building sites in England and had been 'trailing his coat' around the village for days, drunk as a lord and looking for fights. Apparently, he had got his belly-full the previous evening when he had insulted an army gunner in a neighbouring pub and been promptly "butchered on the spot" by the said gunner.

Looking at Ritchie now, I knew he has both truculent and dangerous and when, he offered us a drink we declined with "much thanks". So now, he stood at the bar with his two henchmen, smoking, shouting at everyone at large and drinking rum and blackcurrant "to keep out the wet." He looked a sorry sight. The cheap brown suit was stained and limp. The black eye was green at the edges. A large cut adorned his swollen mouth and his high cheek bone was grazed.

He was glaring at no one in particular when the door opened quietly to admit two very young nuns of the order of "The Little Sisters of the Poor" and they were "on the quest", with small collecting boxes held before them.

They looked fearfully past Ritchie and approached the barman who gave them a shilling out of the till and tuppence out of his pocket. They passed by the two old men and came towards our table. We were delving into our pockets to oblige when Ritchie reeled over and looked malignantly down at the two young girls as we dropped some coins into their boxes.

"Over here, Pat," he bawled, "these two ladies are going to have a drink on me, isn't that so Sister?" he leered.

Pat came up to the bar counter obediently and the little nun said, "alright so, you can buy us a drink."

They both put down their collecting boxes on our table and stepped up to the bar beside Ritchie, as he regained what composure he could. Grinning hugely at all and sundry, he threw a pound note on the bar counter and said quietly, "what'll it be girls?"

The little nun replied without blinking, "two large Powers, please." The barman blanched visibly and Ritchie crowed, "fill 'em up Pat, bejazus, I never saw a nun drunk yet."

Pat placed the two large whiskies on the bar with a glass of water and set up Ritchie's glass beside them. A hush fell on the room as we watched the little nun pick up her glass without adding water and her companion did likewise. They turned to face Ritchie as he absently raised his glass, his battered face wore a bewildered look.

"Good luck and God bless you," said the nuns in unison.

"Aye, good luck," said Ritchie, downing his by now badly needed rum and black. As he did so, the nun produced a bottle from the pocket of her robes, and her friend produced a small funnel and placed it in the neck of the bottle and, while we watched, the two glasses were emptied into the bottle, the cork replaced and the lot disappeared under the robes.

In the silence which followed the nuns picked up their little boxes, smiled angelically at everyone, said "God bless you all," and left!

Note:

The Little Sisters of the Poor cared exclusively for old people in their many convents and hospitals throughout Ireland and accepted any kind of donation which would contribute to the comfort and well being of their patients.

The Mobile Cinema

1947

In March 1947 I went into partnership 50/50 with my brother David J. Cronin, to form a company, which would be known as "**C Mobile Pictures**". The proposition was to bring cinema to all the villages within a ten mile radius of Waterford, where we figured people were starved for entertainment. To this end we purchased the following:

1 Baby Ford Car (Taxed and Insured)	£170.0.0
1 Film Projector and Sound Equipment	£248.0.0
Total	£418.0.0

We booked the Fisherman's Hall, Dunmore East for one night per week at a rent of 30/-. Our film rental was £8 to £10 per week and we rented on a weekly basis as we intended booking five more halls almost immediately. Our first show was on March 4th 1947. However, when we went to book the other halls, we found that they were not on mains electricity. We ran on one show per two weeks and then we got a second hall in Passage East. We got a third hall in Slieverue, a fourth in Piltown, a fifth in Glenmore and a sixth in Portlaw. The venue in Piltown faded out after our third week there, so we had a circuit of 5 halls left. Half of these halls had no electricity, so we had to buy the following:

One 1000 Watt Generator – Deposit	£50.0.0
Delivery and Insurance	£14.0.0
1 Van to carry Generator (Net)	£195.0.0
Insurance and cost of fitting out the van	£34.0.0
Total	£293.0.0.

In June we were doing fairly well, and we rented an office at 11 Blackfriars, over Fennells Barber Shop. A legal agreement and cost of painting and first week's rent at £4.6.8, came to £25. About this time we took on a helper at 15/- a week as there was quite a lot of physical work involved in setting up each night and taking down the screen, the lighting where applicable, packing all equipment into the van etc. There was no seating in half the halls, and we had to supply same – mostly long benches – which had to be stored and stacked each night. We ran a full six-night circuit by mid-July and we had opened a joint current account, putting in £13 each – total £26 – into which all takings were lodged.

On August 8th we lost a hall, due to a disagreement with the landlord, and we got another one at the end of that month. Then a bombshell hit us. Government tax on our ticket – we had to buy rolls of taxed tickets – went up from 10% to 25%, and since we could not pass on the increase, we lost heavily and had to borrow £100 from our father to keep going.

At this point, following burning much midnight oil going through the Entertainment Act and its Statutory Instruments, we discovered that if more than 50% of a performance was live entertainment, you were no longer liable for Tax.

Immediately, we hired six pianos and installed them in the various halls and advertised "Cine-Variety" – live performance from 5 p.m. to 7.30 p.m., and film show from 8 p.m. to 10.15 p.m. David and I supplied the live part by playing piano non-stop in relays from 5 p.m. to 7.30 p.m.

It was customary for the Tax Inspector to visit our halls and check the numbers on our ticket rolls – and books were kept to enable him to see what had been sold and also spot check the audience to see that everybody had got a ticket.

Well, when he arrived he found us playing to an empty hall, but we were open on time to support our advertisement and we got away with it. Incidentally, after we had come up with that solution, all the big cinemas in the town followed suit, and had scrap bands playing for a period exceeding the film time.

As winter arrived, we hit another big snag – there was no heating in our halls and bit by bit attendances dropped off and we finally closed down the business on the 4th February 1948.

We had drawn approximately £80 each out of the business between July and February, and after repaying our debts and selling off all the equipment – mostly at a loss – we had £150 left, which we split 50/50.

We had worked like slaves while the business was going, as jobs were impossible to find at that time and there was little alternative. I was in digs at the time and was selling off my wardrobe to keep going, and had made up my mind to emigrate. When on April 3rd I quite fortuitously got a job with Irish National Insurance Co. as a clerk at the handsome salary of £3.15.5 per week, and I was very glad of that job I can tell you. I stayed with that company for the next 33 years and wound up as General Manager and Director.

The Ferguson Tractor

1948

ACT I

It was the first Monday of the month, "a Fair Day" in Waterford, and the Hill of Ballybricken was a hive of activity. "The Hill" was an open space with the Bull Post standing roughly in the centre of a 250 yard triangle. The perimeter was lined with small shops, and houses interspersed. Most of the shops faced north, and most of the better houses faced south. Two of the largest pubs faced south also, and consequently enjoyed whatever sun there might be.

Corcoran knew from long tightly held experience how important it was to stand your cattle on the sunny side, and when he woke his son Willie at three o'clock that morning he was already planning his strategy. They had to walk the bunch of white faced cattle eight miles to Waterford, and he knew only too well the folly of driving the animals too hard and having them arrive exhausted and looking limp and God forsaken in the cold dawn light. No, he told himself, start early, bring them along nice and handy, rest them and let them get a drink at the stream in Callaghan and get them to the sunny corner in Ballybricken near the first pub at the rise of ground.

Oh, Corcoran knew his business alright – two days before the fair he had moved those cattle into the old four acre field behind the house. The grass was long there and the ditches thick for shelter, and the beasts ate well in the heavy grass, which also cleaned their legs and hooves.

The cattle looked well now as the sun topped the hill and Corcoran knew it, and the best of luck attended him with the arrival right opposite of that "Mane little ferret", O'Toole, with his four dirty old worn out cows, and two of them with only one horn apiece. The contrast was perfect and he stood there quietly and patiently with Willie; his son, and his seven white faced bullocks … and they waited.

Willie was leaning over the back of a bullock, watching the road to the main shopping area when he spotted his man. Corcoran had his back to the lamp post at the corner, looking the other way.

"Watch out, Father" said Willie, "Cooper the butcher is comin' straight for ye."

Corcoran never moved as he replied "Tighten up them beasts now boy, and get their heads up." Willie deftly obliged.

Cooper advanced up the hill to the fair, his eye scanning, sorting and marking automatically as he surveyed the scene.

He had his own reasons for heading in Corcoran's direction – it was a sunny corner where you could stay and talk harmless blather to whoever was there, while you checked and spotted what was on offer, and anyway, the thought of a nice hot whiskey by the fire in the corner pub had filled his mind as he drew near the lamp post.

Corcoran's heavy voice cut through his vision –

"Willie, go over and tell Mr. Molloy I haven't all day to wait."

Willie, well schooled, headed off through the crowd towards Molloy's Butcher shop where he would buy a pound of beef sausages, wait in the shop, and "rush" back with the news.

"He's gone to the railway, Father!" Just as Cooper was engaging Corcoran senior in what might be regarded as civil discourse.

Cooper opened – "A hardy morning there."

"'Tis nearly dinner time," parried Corcoran "and I can tell you there's no bargains left this time of day." Willie glowed with admiration as his father casually stepped on to the footpath while speaking, making himself a foot taller than his adversary.

Cooper mentally slaughtered, quartered and weighed the seven beasts with a glance as he replied, stepping up easily beside Corcoran "Ye know, there's nothin' here today only small, miserable little beasts... no good at all for a butcher."

Corcoran bristled "Yer not by any chance callin' them cattle miserable, are ye?"

"Ah not at all me dear man, sure I was sayin' only the other day that a mejum size bullock could have his place in a butcher's shop – although they have a lot of bone, ye know like." Cooper said easily.

Willie had gone back to leaning on the nearest bullock – he sensed the line tightening between the two, but as yet he couldn't make out who had hooked who, so he concentrated on watching the rivulets of urine and dung which flowed along the gutter between his boots.

"Keep your head down boy" he told himself "and don't distract the oul' fella while he's puttin' manners on the butcher." He was not, however, prepared for what came next as Corcoran displayed his mental agility.

"Ye know," he said looking straight into Cooper's eyes, which were watering slightly with the cold, "I owe you an apology."

"For what?" said Cooper, completely mystified.

Corcoran hung his head ever so slightly and tapped the toe of his boot with his stick and said in a quiet voice "I was at your wife's first cousin's funeral three weeks ago, and I couldn't get near ye with all them big shot cattle dealers that was there, and I was sayin' to the wife goin' home "God dammit ye know, I'm friends with John Cooper these years and many a good beast I sold him and he was always a decent man to deal with and here I am now goin' home and never even bought the man a drink, will you have a hot whiskey with me now to make amends and never mind the cattle?"

Cooper hadn't a hope, and he knew it. They disappeared into the pub, and the deal was done. He gave Corcoran twenty pounds less than the cattle were worth, and Corcoran gave him back a fiver for luck, as he knew full well he had got twenty pounds more than he really expected.

He turned his benevolent eye on the steaming glass as Cooper faded to the doorway — "Good look" he murmured as the door closed.

ACT II

Corcoran leaned back and belched profoundly. Nobody in the crowded pub noticed. Half an hour had passed since Cooper had left with Willie to take the cattle down to the yard behind the butcher's shop.

A third hot whiskey had warmed him down to his toes. He had sent a kid across to the far side of the fairground to bring back three hot crubeens from the huckster's shop which specialized in that delicacy. Two of these glutinous morsels he ate ravenously, and having carefully thrown the bones in the fireplace, he wiped his fingers and face in the newspaper wrapping, and delicately rolled up the remaining one in the rest of the newspaper to keep it warm for Willie. Then he opened the top button of his flap, paid for a large bottle of stout and sighed contentedly as he fondled the roll of notes in the inside pocket of his waistcoat under folded arms.

Willie's mind was soaring with speculation as to what he might do with the half note Cooper had given him for helping with the cattle as he strolled back to the pub. He was feeling hungry now, thirsty too as the sweet smell of stout reached him. Just then there was a hand on his arm –

"Hello there Willie, I heard ye sold the cattle and I'm hopin' to see yer father." It was Jim Kirwan the tractor salesman.

"He's inside in the pub here," said Willie, "come on, I'll find him for ye."

They turned in to the pub and Kirwan took his arm again, "Here, Willie" he smiled, "you're a go ahead man – you wouldn't mind having a nice new Ferguson Tractor now, would ye?" But before Willie could answer his father's voice cut through the smoky air and Willie detected an almost jovial note in it.

"Over here Willie, boy, pull a large stout there for me son will ye, sit down, sit down, here's a crubeen for ye boy, ye must be hungry." And looking at Kirwan he continued "Ah God save us all look what the cat brought in."

"Could I see ye Mr. Corcoran?" Kirwan ventured.

"Of course ye can boy," replied Corcoran, "as long as yer not trying to sell me one of them cursed Fergusons – what are ye havin' anyway?"

"A Lemonade thanks," said Kirwan. Corcoran looked at him pityingly and said loudly "If ye want to talk to a man, ye better be a man – give him a small stout there Miss."

The stout arrived and the three sat down. Willie tackled the crubeen with enthusiasm and Kirwan tried vainly to control the foam rising rapidly in his glass as he poured the stout with an unpractised hand. He cursed his plight as he saw Corcoran wink hugely at Willie. "I heard ye got a right good price for the cattle Mr. Corcoran, and more o'that to ye," said Kirwan raising his froth filled glass – "Good luck – good luck" they chorused and drank.

After a pause Kirwan said "The new Ferguson is only £375 for cash."

"Well now that's very interesting" said Corcoran "for anyone that would be buying one, but of course I always used horses and me sons the same. We have a right good breed of a horse out our way ye know. He'd be a sort of an Irish draught with a dash of the Clydesdale in him and he'd pull anything." Another pause as Corcoran rested on his oars and waited.

"'Tis getting right expensive to keep horses shod nowadays," said Kirwan studying his glass. Willie was lifting his chin to nod his agreement when the boot hit him on the ankle bone. He froze and looked at the fire.

"Not when we does it ourselves" lied Corcoran defiantly.

"I heard right enough, that a blacksmith can hardly make a living anymore." said Kirwan as he watched the colour rising in Corcoran's face. "But" he added quickly, raising his voice to be heard by others, "I suppose it's because really the ould horse is finished in the farms. Sure 'twould take ye all day to bring a churn of milk to the creamery and your day would be gone for nothing. And sure with the tractor you could be in and back in an hour and not only bring in yer own churn, but carry in the churn for a neighbour, maybe, who wouldn't be so lucky or maybe wouldn't have the price of a Ferguson."

"Faith then" said Corcoran, raising his already big voice, "I heard on good authority that them tractors are no good on hilly land and ye could get kilt off of 'em."

"Only in the hands of an amachure," said Kirwan, his voice rising.

"An' there's another thing," rapped Corcoran, "tractors cost money from once you bring 'em into the yard 'till ye get rid of 'em – with oil and repairs and God knows what else – when with the horse ye have his diet for nothin' and his manure for the land in return and he'll work away for ye and even if he drops dead, ye have his carcase to sell to the knacker man for a pound or two."

Ears were cocked all around the pub now as the combatants circled mentally, seeking an opening. There was a hush while glasses were raised and stout was sipped carefully. Kirwan drained his drink, put down the glass and stood up wiping his mouth.

"That's all history Mr. Corcoran" he said "an' I'll tell ye what, I'll bring out a Ferguson to your farm on Friday at ten o'clock and give ye a free trial and demonstration and you'll see for yerself that any damn thing your horse can do, my tractor will do it better." He held out his hand across the table to Corcoran and they shook hands. "Thanks for the drink and Good luck, I'll see ye Friday. So long Willie."

"Ay, good luck Jim" said Willie.

Kirwan picked his way towards the door unhurriedly with all eyes on him. "That shook the oul' bastard" he told himself as he buttoned his gabardine. He was one step short of the door when Corcoran's voice called out.

"Hey Kirwan, I didn't ever hear of a Ferguson having a foal." The door slammed and bawdy laughter followed the salesman down the street.

Postscript:

Within ten years the horse was gone from the farm, but here and there you would see an odd one. I think that Corcoran's was one such place.

The Fair, Ballybricken - before the tractor!
From a photo by A. H. Poole, Waterford

Whiskey And Its Disciples

1949

In the thirties you could get several kinds of whiskey in the pubs of Ireland but the brands which dominated the market were Powers, Jameson and Paddy. These were manufactured by three separate and distinct firms, Paddy being made in Cork and the other two in non-Cork locations, – far off places like Dublin.

Competition between the firms was lively and each had its own Travellers – nowadays called "Reps" – who covered the country booking orders, collecting accounts and most importantly, maintaining customer relations.

Brand loyalty was most marked in Cork and any self respecting Corkman would not be seen drinking anything but Paddy. Nevertheless, all three brands were widely sold because each one had a distinctive taste and a definite tradition. For example, Jameson was considered to be a sort of Protestant whiskey, Powers would be a good middle of the road Irish Catholic whiskey and Paddy was a CORK whiskey. Of course, there were plenty, more than enough some would say, of Corkmen in Dublin and a Dubliner heard ordering a Paddy, maybe because he liked the flavour, knew in his heart that he ran a serious risk of being mistaken for a Cork man. Such was the frame which surrounded the following story told to me by a good Corkman at a late night drinking party in Dublin.

Three commercial travellers representing respectively Powers, Jameson and Paddy were in the habit of meeting in a Cork hostelry whenever their paths crossed on their regular journeys to that city. The spirit of the meeting was one of friendly rivalry and much useful information was exchanged – who was a good payer or a bad one, who was going where next week, what was happening within the industry etc. It was usually a short meeting, since each had his calls to do, and only one round of drinks would be bought, each taking it in his turn to buy. Needless to say, they all drank whiskey and, of course, each would be expected to drink his own product and support his own firm.

On this particular day, it fell to the Powers rep to stand the round of drinks and he stood up to the bar and ordered three half ones, a Power, a Jameson and a Paddy. But, as he finished, the Paddy rep said, "hold on a minute there, I'll have a Jameson this time!"

Deeply questioning eyes impaled the Cork man as the drinks came to the table. Water was carefully added and the first sip was taken with a subdued, "Good Luck." Glasses were put down and cigarettes lit in silence, all eyes still searching the Corkman.

A second sip was interrupted by the Powers man. "Be God, you're a right man to be travellin' for Paddy and you not even drinkin' yer own product. What the hell are ye at at-all?"

The Paddy man downed the last of his Jameson and flicked his cigarette ash in the general direction of the ash tray before answering.

"Well now, I'll tell 'oo. I have and appointment in ten minutes to meet a very important customer and I wouldn't want to have the smell of drink offa me, goin' in there!"

The Dance Scene

1950

In the 1940s, in Waterford, dancing was popular with young and middle-aged alike and was where boy met girl.

There were several dance halls, the principal one being the *Olympia Ballroom*, which had originally been a roller skating rink. Situated in Parnell Street it had a maple floor and could hold about twelve hundred dancers.

Next was the *Large Room* at the Town Hall, on The Mall. This was upstairs in the Municipal building which also held the Theatre Royal, one of the oldest purpose-built theatres in Ireland, dating back to the mid eighteenth century. The "Large Room," as it was popularly known, had a pine floor which was regarded as the best in Waterford for dancing. It was said that you could dance all night on that floor and not feel tired – and having danced many a night there I would have to agree. Last but not least was the *Red Cross Ballroom*, over Burtons, in Michael Street.

These three places were the venues for the main social occasions such as the Hunt Ball, The Beagle Ball, The Military Ball, The Red Cross Ball, etc. Incidentally, functions like the Hunt Ball were known as Dress Dances, which meant white tie & tails (or dinner jacket) for the men and Ball Gowns for the ladies, and ran from 10 p.m. to 4 a.m. with supper included. Admission would be ten shillings to twenty one shillings for the most prestigious and there would be a bar.

There were also four lesser venues: the *LSF Hall* (local Security Force), in William Street – now Keighrey's Furniture Store – which emerged during the war; *The Regal*, in Thomas Street; The *"Tubs of Blood"* at the junction of the Glen and Thomas street, and the *NUR Hall* (National Union of Railwaymen) over Hill's Salt Store in O'Connell's Street. Incidentally, The "Tubs" was where the soldiers went and fights were not infrequent there, hence the name!

My first venture into the band business was in 1943, when I formed a four piece outfit – two accordions, drums and myself on piano – and I rented the "Regal" from the then owner, a man called Mullins, who had a dance licence for the hall. The rent for the hall was thirty shillings for the month and I charged one shilling and sixpence per head for admission. I also had to hire a piano, plus a cashier for the door. My career in that location was short and sweet. The opening night was packed, the second night was half full and things got progressively worse and eventually it faded out and I had to close down.

My enthusiasm had overtaken my judgement. Had I done my sums properly I'd have realised that dances, though popular, would only succeed if (a) Sponsored by a club and (b) if held on either Friday or Saturday. No dance hall could hope to run seven nights a week – and with the same band. Anyway, it was a relatively cheap lesson and I put it down to experience.

For the record the two accordionists were "Togo" Quigley and Jimmy (Fitzy) Fitzgerald and the drummer was Pierre (The Gunner) White.

❧

At this time the people who "fronted" dance bands in Waterford were; Mick O'Shea, Busty Griffin, Billy Tuohy, Hugh Dunphy, Frank King, "Pop" Walsh, Big Tom O'Brien, Billy Fahy, Geoff Cronin, Dick Cronin, Paddy Rafferty and Sadie Byrne.

The Musicians working in those years were:

Sax	Big Tom, Paddy Rafferty, Ken McKinnon, Johnny Bourke, Eddie Carroll, Jimmy Power, Tommy McGrath, Dick Cooper, Billy Fahy (Clarinet), Harry Martin.
Trumpets	Johnny O'Connell, Monty Clooney, Johnny Whelan, Charlie McGrath, Frankie King.

Drums	Davy O'Brien, Pierre White, Billy Hayes, Eamon Phelan, Michael Cahill, Sean Mulcahy, Algy Fitzgerald, Eric Bremner.
Guitar	Des Manahan, Val Doonican, Bruce Clarke
Double Bass	Dick Dunphy, Paddy Kavanagh, Ernie Mosyer, Geoff Cronin.
Accordion	Drohan Brothers, Sadie Byrne, Mick O'Shea, Geoff Cronin, Dick Cronin, Billy Twohy, Busty Griffin, Jackie Chester, Jimmy Fitzgerald.
Piano	Gerry Dunne, Bruce Clarke, Geoff Cronin, Joe Manahan, Ned Roche, Martin Sullivan, Claus Cantwell, Paschal Kennedy, Maudie Tuohy.
Trombone	Derek Hyder
Vocals	Ena Galvin, Johnny Hodgers,

Apart from the above there may have been others which have escaped my memory. Also, I have not included the members of the Royal Showband who were just emerging as I was exiting the scene in 1962. By that time I had been in and out of the music business for the previous eighteen years or so and my experiences over the period would fill a book – a large one! I can, however, give you a "brief" outline of what went on.

❧

To begin with I played piano with "The Hep Cats", a six-piece formed by my brother Dick. When he went into partnership with Paddy Rafferty and the band became Paddy

Rafferty's I continued on Piano and eventually got fired because I could only read guitar symbols.

A short time afterwards I went back to that outfit on Double Bass and did a year with them. Meantime, Dick and I, plus drummer, did a lot of gigs in hotels as a three-piece, with me on piano.

Then Dick went to Dublin and played with Phil Murtagh the resident band in the Metropole Ballroom. He later went on to become a chemist and emigrated to Canada. At almost the same time I went to work in Dublin and did a year's apprenticeship in Confectionary at the Swiss Chalet in Merion Row – without pay! On my return to Waterford I picked up a job with a "scrap" four-piece outfit and played for the summer season in the Tara Ballroom – May to September – in Courtown Harbour, Co. Wexford.

While living in Dublin I also pursued an interest in Ballroom Dancing which had begun when I took lessons from Irene Murray in Waterford – she had a school of dancing at the top end of Colbeck Street. In Dublin I went to the Graham School of Dancing where I took my Bronze Medal and Silver Medal. It was there also that I took my first course of study to become a teacher of Ballroom Dancing.

For various reasons I became disenchanted with the Graham tuition and I moved on to the Evelyn Burchill School where I finished my studies and passed the exam for Associateship of the National Association of Teachers of Dancing, which I got with a commendation – ANATD Comm – and also got the associateship of the

Imperial Society of Teachers of Dancing – AISTD. These qualifications enabled me to teach, which I had in fact been doing while a student in both the schools. All this was hard going and meant that in addition to my day job (8 a.m. to 5 p.m.) I was dancing every night of the week as well. It took all my spare time.

On my return to Waterford, however, all sorts of other things happened to interrupt my music "career". First I tackled the bakery business, which my father had, and set about converting a bread trade into a confectionary business. This involved stripping down the existing bakehouse, selling off all the machinery, building a new bakehouse on

Summer season in the New Ballroom in Courtown Harbour.
Left to Right - Jimmy Power (Alto Sax) Mikey Denn (Drums), Jimmy Fitzgerald (accordion), G. Cronin (Piano).

a site behind the shop, building a new double-deck oven and getting new equipment installed. But just as I was preparing to launch the new venture the bank foreclosed and my father was forced to sell No. 12 John Street – it went for just £3,000!

Having received my share of the proceeds, around £400, I went into partnership with my younger brother David and we set up a mobile cinema outfit – which is the subject of a separate story.

When I returned to the Band game, a year and a half later, it was to form a three-piece – Piano, Alto Sax and Drums – and I played the first dance at The Haven Hotel, Dunmore East. This outfit grew to a four-piece and at a later stage became the resident band at the Haven when Dinner Dances became the rage and spread to the Grand Hotel Tramore, and the Majestic Hotel Tramore.

In tandem with this I ran a seven-piece band and got regular bookings at the Olympia Waterford and also the Collins Hall Clonmel, The Mayfair Kilkenny, The Town Hall Dungarvan and all points in between. On occasion I strengthened the outfit to nine pieces – Vocalist, Piano, Bass, Drums, two Alto Saxes, one Tenor Sax, and two Trumpets.

The dance scene in Ireland at this time was really swinging, to the point that it was rumoured that Bands from England would soon be coming to cash-in on the Irish market. This idea, when I thought about it, seemed quite possible and took root in my head. While I was still thinking about it I had a visit from the then Chairman of the Irish Federation of Musicians, Paddy Malone, and the General Secretary, Paddy Donaghue, who confirmed that certain promoters in Dublin had already booked the top English Bands to tour Ireland.

On the spot we formed the Waterford branch of the Irish Federation of Musicians, and I enrolled all the members of my bands – I being the Secretary of the new branch of the "Fed", as this powerful Trade Union was known. The Fed was going to insist that a Fed band would have to be engaged as support to any imported band appearing in Ireland.

BAND PARADE   By Gay

GEOFFREY CRONIN

DAVY O'BRIEN

ANDY SMITH

The Geoffrey Cronin Trio is the up-to-date combination which plays strict tempo dance music at such well-known hotels as the Grand, Tramore, and the Haven, Dunmore.

Times Pictorial,
Week ending July 8th, 1950.

Well, nothing happened for some months and although I tried to get other bands interested I did not succeed because people thought it wouldn't happen, and if it did the Union would be unable to enforce the arrangement.

Meanwhile, a Sax player, whom I knew, had come back

157

from England and settled in Waterford. He was Big Tommy O'Brien and he promptly formed his own band and got some bookings. I didn't mind much until he began poaching some of my musicians and this I *did* mind because I had the best of them.

We were "daggers drawn" for a time and a regular

Early 1950s Trio at Haven Hotel. Left to right - Eddie Carroll (alto sax), Pierre White, "The Gunner" (drums) , Self (on piano).

vendetta ensued. This got neither of us anywhere and when I realised this I went to see him and we came to an "arrangement". He would "join" my band and I would "join" his! – only it would be the same band! The difference would be that if he got the booking he would stand up and lead the "Big Tom Band" and I would sit down and If I got the booking I would lead the "Geoff Cronin Band" and he would sit down.

Self on accordion at the Haven Hotel late 1950.
NB. The piano needed tuning

In this way, I gained a top class Alto player and he had the best pianist on the local scene. The public never spotted this move and both of us did well, as we split the leader's fee.

When the big English bands finally arrived we got ALL the support work, as the "Fed" had won their battle and we were the only "Fed" band in the area. We played support to such famous names as Jack Parnell, Harry Roy, Sid Phillips and many others.

On one memorable occasion we had a great laugh when Geraldo came to town with his 26-piece orchestra. He appeared at the Olympic Ballroom and the admission was five shillings. The attendance was about 1,200 people and during the dance my "fans" put up posters all around the hall advertising the Dunmore East Sailing Club Dress Dance, Music by the Geoff Cronin Trio – Admission 21 shillings!

To add insult to injury, at the end of the dance when Geraldo stood majestically on the band-stand, cigar in hand, preparing to sign autographs and I was at the other end of the stand merely collecting my gear, a crowd of my fans gathered in front of me screaming for my autograph and waving programmes in my face! It was a total send-up and Geraldo looked shocked and amazed. What a laugh we had.

Saturday Night at the Haven Hotel, Dunmore East -
Summer 1959

As time went on I progressed in my day job and pressure of work, among other factors, led me to wind up the seven-piece. I continued, however, with the four-piece, doing just the Haven and the other hotels plus small club dances at the weekend. I also formed a different quartet to perform at the local Jazz Club concerts in the Municipal Theatre. In my "Spare time" I also set up a Barbershop Quartet just for fun. I called it "The Time Travellers" and it was quite successful. The members of the quartet were Eamon Phelan, Donal Gough, Des Manahan and myself.

The last performance of my band was in 1962 and though it had all been tough going I enjoyed every minute of it.

At this moment I have been approached (at the age of 81!) to play Accordion in a new "Tango Orchestra"! Tango, and indeed Ballroom Dancing in general, are currently enjoying a revival. What Next??

Retention

1951

In Ireland in the 1930s, a large proportion of the population was engaged in farming, and even though the country was in the throes of "the economic war" with Britain, and though it was extremely hard for a farmer to scrape a living, his hunger for the land had not been diminished.

Land was the source of income by tradition, and consequently, he who had the land also had power in the family, and ultimately control. It was no surprise, therefore, that a farmer would be slow, and even reluctant to make over the place to his son. The custom was that he would make his Will, or relinquish his grip on the farm, only when he was on his death bed.

In the thatched farmhouse, the mood was sombre and strained. The woman, her son in his forties, and two close relatives sat in silence. "Himself" was upstairs, dying.

The doctor had left saying "He has retention Ma'am and he can't last long." The priest had come and anointed the man and the solicitor had been summoned to make the Will. The two relatives would be the witnesses.

The Solicitor came and without delay went upstairs, drew up the Will, had it signed and witnessed, and came downstairs. He was then seated at the kitchen table and was offered the hospitality of the house – tea, home-made bread and jam.

"You wanted to ask me something" the Solicitor said when he had sipped the strong tea.

The woman looked uneasy, and a slight flush came to her face. She swallowed hard and said "Tell me, Sir, in plain language, what *is* retention?"

Now it was his turn to look uneasy, but he took a deep breath and said "Well Ma'am, it means that he can't pass water."

Immediately, the woman rose and walked slowly to the open doorway, where she stood, sobbing gently. As the Solicitor approached, she turned to him with tears running down her face. "Ah the poor fellow, God help him," she said. "I mind the time he could stand here on this threshold, and hit the cow house door on the far side of the yard."

The Haul Of Bass

1955

One June afternoon in the '50s I was travelling home from Clonmel – I was "on the road" for Irish National Insurance Company at the time – and my last call of the day was in Carrick-on-Suir. A I was coming back in the car after making the call, I stopped at Francie Mullins fishing tackle shop and saw a cheap fishing rod in the window.

"It's made out of a tank aerial" he told me, "and I got a dozen of them from a fella dealin' in surplus war materials. A handy little rod," he said, "ideal for spinning. Here," he said, "let me put a spinning reel on it and you'll see how well it feels."

He did so, and when I picked it up it just felt right in my hand.

"You could cast with that for the day and your wrist wouldn't get tired ", he continued. "And here's what I'll do with you, a hundred yards of nylon line, a German bait, the rod and the reel, the lot for a five pound note. What do you say?"

"Done," I said, handing over the last fiver I had in this world.

As I drove home, I felt a whole new phase of my life opening up. Having been brought up by the sea, I knew all about fishing, but since getting married, I had been unable to afford the tackle etc. and at this stage, I dearly wanted to teach my sons all I knew about fishing. When I got home and told my wife about my purchase, she saw the possibilities in terms of food for the table and it was decided to try out the new rod that very evening.

So, after dinner, leaving our eldest daughter to babysit, my wife and I set off for Saleen, near Tramore, where a deep sea inlet, called the *Rinnashark*, came in by a

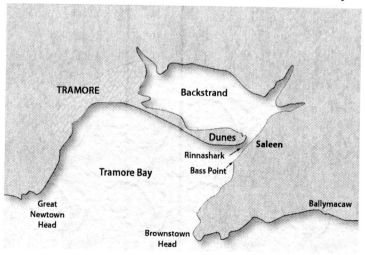

long beach. It was known to be a good spot for Bass fishing and at that time, perhaps in July or August, shoals of Bass would come inshore on occasion and provide good sport for anyone who happened to be fishing at the time. However, I was not trying to catch anything that evening as the tide was low and it was a bit early in the season. I just wanted to try casting with the new rod and to get used to the feel of it.

Anyway, on arrival at Saleen I set up the rod and as it was a fine June evening, we decided to walk out along the beach to a place called Bass Point, almost a quarter of a mile distant. When we got to the spot, I made my first cast, which fell short of the channel and as I retrieved the bait, it stopped suddenly.

"Damn it" I said, "I'm caught in the weeds."

The next second, the rod nearly jumped out of my hand and the reel sang, I was into a heavy fish and he was heading for deep water.

I put on the brake and began to play him. I didn't think the line would hold, but taking him gently, I had him on the beach in ten minutes.

It was a beautiful Bass, easily seven pounds weight. I was elated and couldn't wait to make another cast. Again, it fell short of the deep water, and as I wound in the bait, I knew this time I was stuck in the weeds. I gave a hard pull and the water exploded as another huge Bass broke the surface and headed out at speed for the deep channel. I checked him just before he got there, and I eased him down the beach into the slack water, where I beached him. It was a Bass a little smaller than the first one, and though I fished on for another half hour, I caught nothing else.

Meanwhile my wife, Joan, had picked up a stout piece of driftwood and some nylon cord from the beach, and we tied the fish through the gills to the stick and holding an end each, we set out to carry our catch back to the car. It should be noted here that Bass normally caught in these waters would be two or three pounds weight.

As we started back, we met two men out for a walk and they stopped us to admire our catch. They asked what weight the fish might be, and I said the big one was about seven pounds and the other one about six. There was not another sinner to be seen on the beach in any direction and we met no one else by the time we reached the car. Anyway, we weighed the fish when we got home and the bigger fish turned out to be seven and a half pounds, and the other one weighed six and a quarter. We congratulated ourselves on the catch, and after having a cup of tea and a chat, we retired for the night.

Nest morning I had to go to the bank and while there a friend took me aside and said in a low voice "The Bass are

A haul of Bass!

in at Saleen – two guys were fishing there yesterday, and one guy got seven fish and the other guy got six." He pressed his finger to his lips. When I got back to my office, another man rang me and said he heard that a party fishing at Saleen last night caught seventy-six Bass between them. By lunch time I could be told that two boats had fished Saleen the previous evening, and one boat took seven boxes of Bass and the other one took six. I told my wife all this when I went home to lunch, and she could hardly believe the speed and the ramifications of the angler's grapevine. It was likely that the pair we encountered on the beach had ended up in the local pub, and from there the story had grown not only legs, but wings as well.

By tea time, the rumours were flying to the point where we decided to drive out to Saleen after tea to see what the effect had been. We drove out the high road, which overlooked the beach and there they were, almost thirty or maybe forty anglers standing practically elbow to elbow along the beach, thrashing the water with their lines. We went to the local pub for a drink to quell our laughter, and we heard even more fabulous stories about the biggest shoal of Bass ever seen in Saleen. On our way home we stopped at the car park where weary anglers were packing up, and enquiring if they had any luck heard "No, but there was any amount of Bass here last night!" The miracle of the five loaves and two fishes came to mind, and we laughed all the way home.

The Rosary

1955

On February 16th 1949 I married Joan Flanagan in St. John's Church, Waterford at eight o'clock in the morning. The priest who officiated was Rev. John Flynn, my wife's first cousin, the best man was Jack Flanagan and the bridesmaid was Irene Murray, both first cousins of my wife. I was employed by Irish National Insurance Company Ltd. As a clerk, and my pay was four pounds twelve shillings and seven pence weekly. My wife earned three pounds a week working as a book-keeper in Jack Flanagan's Fish and Poultry business, and our

rent on 30 St. Ursula's Terrace was nine shillings and six-pence per week.

Pregnancy dictated that my wife quit her job in June of that year, and it soon became obvious that my income would not support us, so I went "moonlighting" as a free-lance pianist for local dance bands. The rates were one pound for an 8-12 dance, and one pound ten shillings – maybe two pounds – for a 9–3.

In time, we moved house to 46 Lr. Newtown, and by 1955 I had my own dance band, still moonlighting, the job was slightly better, and I had four children, but that's another story.

At the outset of our marriage, my wife being a religious woman, it was decided that we should say the family Rosary every day. So, each evening after dinner, the family would kneel down, elbows on chairs, and recite the five decades of the Rosary plus "the trimmings". The latter consisted of prayers for deceased family members, for the souls in Purgatory, for the canonisation of Blessed Martin etc. etc. and took half as long as the Rosary.

But, what with travelling all day and moonlighting until four or five in the morning, the Rosary had a hypnotic effect on me and I would "nod off" after the first decade. I just could not stay awake and only responded with "Holy Mary, Mother of God etc." whenever my wife gave me an elbow in the ribs, which was frequently! She was a pragmatic woman, God rest her, and it was agreed that however short my night's rest would be, I would not be disturbed before 8 a.m., and if any of the children woke during the night, she would get up and attend to them.

I came home one morning about 4.30 a.m. after playing at a dance, fell into bed exhausted, and fell fast asleep immediately. I was not to know that one of the children who was teething had got my wife out of bed five or six times, and she was exhausted too, and her temper not the best. When the child woke again and cried fit to wake the house, she prepared to get up yet again when she beheld me fast asleep and snoring gently.

It was the last straw! She decided that I should be the one to get up and see to the child now crying loudly. To that end, she gave me a smart elbow in the ribs and got the instant response "Holy Mary Mother of God" etc. Well, worn out as she was, that good lady just had to laugh as she resignedly got up and soothed the child, and she told this story many times against me over the years that followed.

Tommy And The Fish

1960

Tommy was a clerk in the office of a large Dublin company and every day he came to work on the Harcourt Street line and returned home by the 5.15 p.m. train on the same line. He lived only a few hundred yards from the Milltown Station and the train passed by the end of his back garden.

On Fridays, it was his custom to call to a fishmonger's in Chatham Street on his way to Harcourt Street Station. There he would collect his standing order of two fillets of plaice, and then proceed to the train. Everything was timed to a nicety, and Tommy would stroll into the station and take his seat by the window as the train pulled out.

Tommy would then sit back and relax, reading his evening paper, and as the train passed the end of his garden, he would casually open the window and throw out the parcel of fish which would land in the centre of his lawn. His wife would then emerge, collect the parcel, retire inside and put the fish on the grill to cook. Meanwhile, Tommy would proceed in leisurely fashion, paper under his arm, and arrive home just as his wife was serving up his tea – one lightly grilled fillet of plaice. Timing really *is* everything!!

Descriptions of a mean man:

"You wouldn't see his heart on a clean plate!"
"If he was a ghost he wouldn't give you a fright."
"He was so mean he'd frame a ha'penny."

The Power Of Prayer

1964

The Bull Ring in Wexford was bounded on one side by the Insurance office and, next door to it, was the Pub, Grocery and Undertakers all under the same roof and proprietorship. This was a source of great interest to tourists and, indeed, a subject of many photographs taken by the said tourists.

At about eleven o'clock in the day the sun would shine (when it shone) up the main street from the south and it would rest on the steps of the Insurance office for half an hour or more in the summer, making it and ideal resting place for some of the locals who didn't mind the fact that the clients of the Insurance Company had to, more or less, climb over them to gain entry to that office.

Jack was one of those locals. He was small, flat-capped and seventy three years of age. He had the old age pension and lived alone in a small terrace house on the hill overlooking the town. He was not a particularly religious man but, after his wife died, he took the habit of walking down to ten o'clock mass in Rowe Street chapel to "say a few prayers for her" and to pass an hour. After mass he would walk down to the main street where he invariably met some of his pals for a quick chat while making his way towards the Bull Ring. Once arrived there he would take his seat on the steps of the Insurance office and have a leisurely smoke, passing the time of day with all and sundry.

Come midday, the Angelus would ring out and he would remove his cap, say the Angelus prayers while checking in his pocket for the price of a small bottle of stout. Having satisfied himself regarding the state of his meagre finances, he would don his cap and stroll next door. The small bottle would last half an hour, stretched by gossip with the landlord about the day's funeral or some other such cheerful subject. At 12.30 Jack would visit the toilet and leave, on his way to his daughter's home for his dinner.

Such was his daily programme. The pension was small in the 1950s and could only be eked out over the week by exercising the most careful and stringent management particularly when it came to the single bottle of stout which he enjoyed so much. No way could he rise to the second bottle or even dream of "standing one" to a pal. Even so, he accepted his lot and counted his blessings.

One particular Thursday morning in June, Jack arrived as usual about eleven o'clock and strolled about the Bullring in thoughtful mood before taking his seat on the steps of the Insurance office. Tomorrow was pension day and today he was flat broke. A neighbour's grandson, who had made his first communion that morning, had been "presented" to him on his way from mass and his last shilling had gone to the expectant child. He did have three cigarettes left, however, and he smoked half of one of these now. Topping it carefully, he blew gently through it to keep it sweet for a relight later on and slipped it into the top pocket of his coat.

Just then the Angelus rang out. Jack remaining seated on the step, removed his cap, blessed himself, holding the cap in front of him in his joined hands he bowed his head and "said" the Angelus. As he flowed into the final prayer, a pair of tourists rounded the corner beside him and, as they passed by, two shiny half crowns landed in his cap!

Jack was very late for his dinner that day!

The Tangler's Hat

1965

In the days when the Fair was the commercial and indeed social life-blood of small towns all over Ireland, certain rules of behaviour became rigidly entrenched in the process of buying and selling in the market place. One sacrosanct rule dictated that if a buyer was in negotiation with a seller, no third party could interrupt. Transgression of this rule usually resulted in a split head at the very least – and anyone who went to a fair was very much aware of this.

In the structure of the fair, the main groups were the sellers and the buyers, but between the two, there was a well defined slot occupied by the "middle man" known to both sides as "the Tangler". He worked on commission, for either side and sometimes both. He had power too, for he could keep a seller occupied in useless conversation thereby keeping the sale "open" long enough for the Tangler's chosen buyer to arrive and take over the negotiations. He was regarded as a smart operator and his presence was not always welcome. Nevertheless, where there was a fair, there you could find a tangler and many of them dressed "like their betters," adopting the bowler hat as a badge of office with the short rain coat, polished leather leggings and boots serving to underline the classification.

The method of transporting small animals such as pigs, sheep, goats etc. was to carry them in a specially adapted horse or pony cart. Wooden creels would be lashed together and placed vertically on the cart and then tied down at the corners so that the result looked like a wooden cage tumbril fashion – about three feet off the base of the cart.

The story which follows and which is "sworn true" was told to me in the 1960s by a friend I shall call "Pat".

There was a fair on one day towards the middle of April in the town of Enniscorthy and it was a fairly busy fair with a good share of stock being sold. Pigs had gone very well and by around nine o'clock in the day there were very few left.

A butcher, of enormous size, had bought several lots of porkers and he now turned his attention to a creel of strong pigs heeled up by the '98 monument in the centre of the square. A larger than life bronze statue of a Wexford Pike-man gazed into the distance from the top of the monument, and the Butcher below looked even bigger as he strolled up and leaned his elbows on the top of the creel and eyed the pigs carefully.

At five minutes to nine, the Tangler was on his way down the hill from The Duffry to the Square. He had managed to "stand in" on two small cattle deals, and had collected four pounds for his trouble. He now had a commission to locate five or six good pigs for a dealer who would follow him down in five or ten minutes and he whistled a tune from "Maritana" as he contemplated the prospect of another couple of pounds in his pocket.

The Tangler's bowler hat was tilted slightly down over one eye, his iron shod heels clipped on the pavement in time to his tune and as he arrived at the edge of the square, he turned back the collar of his raincoat and scanned the scene.

As he picked his way among the pens of fowl and knots of sheep, he paused deliberately to examine a tidy Welsh pony with exaggerated care and passing a bawdy observation with the owner, he felt good, damn good. Four pounds in your pocket felt good – the money gave him a feeling bordering on recklessness. Whilst appearing to examine the pony, his eye, practised and accurate, had homed in on the creel of clean, firm pigs by the monument, the same which was now adorned by the huge butcher, deep in parley with the owner of the pigs.

The tangler walked on, surveying the scene. As he turned the corner and faced the square from the far end, he spotted his dealer lighting his pipe, and signalled him by straightening his bowler. The dealer leaned back against the wall and puffed his pipe in reply. The tangler made two passes by the monument, on his mettle now to separate the butcher from the owner of the pigs. The butcher never stirred. He seemed not to notice the tangler, edging around on the blind side of the pillar, trying desperately to catch the owner's eye, and to dislodge him from the conversation.

It was no good, try as he might, he could not get an opening. He backed off and stood on the footpath stamping his foot noisily to remove "something" from his boot. The dealer gazed straight at him and tapped out his pipe on the wall. He would not wait much longer now.

Suddenly the tangler moved, his mind made up. He stamped noisily towards the creel of pigs, banging his legging with his cane. As he drew level the owner looked round, the tangler took a quick breath and said "How much is he offering you anyway?"

A sudden hush fell on the scene and the tangler decided to walk on. His second step was about to hit the ground when a massive pair of hands picked him up by the front of his coat and slammed his back hard against the creel. His head swam as all the breath left his body and as the hands held him there, the butcher's huge head was lowered to level with the tangler's face.

"Lookit here you," snorted the butcher, "if you don't fuck off outa here, I'll put the brim of that hat around yer balls wood a clatter."

He released his grip and the ashen-faced tangler slid to the ground amid the dung and feathers of a fowl pen.

At this point in the story, I tried to visualize the operation outlined by the butcher. I failed and said to Pat "Just how, exactly, could this happen?"

He smiled and said "Aw bejazes it could happen alright, you'd want to see that butcher deliver an uppercut."

Description of a poor salesman
"He couldn't sell ice-cream in Hell!"

The Turkey Run

1968

"Inspector of Agents" was the grandiose title that Tim had. He worked for a prestigious general insurance company based in Dublin and his function was to call on established Agents of the company in order to develop business introduced by those agents, to collect their accounts, to handle their claims and generally foster the interests of the company. He also had to promote good relations with the more important clients in his area.

A client in this latter category happened to be an exporter of poultry and poultry products who had his business in a town some thirty miles from Dublin. Over the years Tim, who provided exemplary service to his clients, became on friendly terms with him and on a routine P.R. call, around Christmas, he was presented with a turkey – free of charge. Not only that, but the client told Tim if any of his colleagues required a turkey for Christmas they could avail of a substantial discount on same.

Tim's colleagues were given this news, but on a very limited basis – close friends only! Come Saturday, two such friends accompanied him on a trip to the turkey store where, true to his word, the poulterer did the needful and they returned with two fine birds at practically half price. Such was their gratitude that they stood Tim a pub lunch and a couple of tinctures as well.

The following Easter Tim had four colleagues in his car as they drove to the turkey store where they were again cordially received and four turkeys were brought home in triumph.

They had stopped on the way down for a "jar" – just a quick one – and had another on the way back, followed by a snack and some more "drinkies" after the car was garaged. Tim enjoyed the day and after all he told himself it was "good for business".

During the remainder of that year Tim checked with his client to make sure that he didn't mind being visited by "a few more" of his closest friends, on the understanding that Tim would introduce them personally. He was very relieved when the client raised no objection because news of this turkey "el dorado" had spread rather further around the office than Tim had originally intended.

By the time Christmas was approaching Tim received a rather peremptory note from one of the Head Office department managers, called "Theo", requesting his presence.

This particular manager was, to quote Tim, "a thorny little bastard" whom nobody liked, so he wasn't looking forward to the meeting. He assumed that there had been some complaint about some case or other and he was on edge when he responded to the summons. He was not, however, prepared for the reception he got for he was shown into a chair and offered a cup of coffee. Before he could recover, he was offered a cigarette *and* a light.

Theo smiled affably at the astonished Tim and said "this is not about business Tim." He paused and then continued, "No, it's just that I want to ask you a favour; could I please join in your "Turkey Run?"

Tim was dumfounded and was nodding agreement when Theo added "and could I bring my two Chief Clerks as well?"

Again Tim nodded and left the room in a daze.

Well, to cut to the chase, so to speak, the net result was that two days before Christmas Eve FOUR company cars – eighteen people – left Head Office for the trip to the turkey store. I should add that this was before "drunk driving" was outlawed, which was just as well because this convoy stopped at several hostelries along the way. The Christmas spirit was in full swing and on arrival most of the party was in fine form, including Theo, who was in fact legless and stayed in the car while the turkeys were being purchased.

Such was the gratitude of this party that they insisted on bringing the client "across the road" for a Christmas drink. This process took over an hour and Theo surprised all by joining the company and buying his round and later collecting his turkey.

On the way home they stopped at more inns and a fish & chip shop and yet more drink was consumed. Theo, meanwhile, insisted on keeping his turkey on his lap and was so drunk that one of the lads tied the neck of the turkey to Theo's wrist "so that he wouldn't lose it." (Drunken logic is so crystal clear!) Incidentally, he used the belt off Theo's gabardine to accomplish this task.

The various guys lived in different areas of Dublin and by the time the drivers deciphered the garbled instructions they were getting the hour was getting extremely late. Theo complicated everything by refusing to tell anyone where he lived and oddly enough nobody knew. However, the "committee" of his fellow drunks decided that he *definitely* lived in Harold's Cross, so they dropped him off there at around 2 a.m.... By that time nobody really cared whether he got home or not.

At approximately 4 a.m., accompanied by two policemen, he arrived at his home in Ranelagh – miles from Harold's Cross – where he rang the bell, being incapable of using the key. After a while his wife appeared and seeing the state of him she said "Where in God's name were you till this hour?"

Theo smiled sheepishly and replied with a vestige of dignity "I was getting a turkey my dear."

"What turkey?" she almost shouted.

"This Turkey," he said triumphantly, holding up his right

arm to which there was attached the head and neck of a turkey. That was all that was left of the poor bird, which had been dragged all the way from Harold's Cross to Ranelagh.

The two policemen had found Theo wandering in the streets in the small hours and had found an envelope in his pocket with his name and address.

Later, they recounted their part of the saga to their amused friends and eventually it filtered back to the office where it was forever hotly denied by Theo.

Salad And Omelets

In Kritsa

1975

In 1975 my wife and I had our first continental holiday – two weeks in Crete, self-catering, cost £105. The resort was Aghios Nicholas, one of the island's showpieces situated a short 30 miles from the airport in Heraklion.

It was the month of May and the sea was still cold, so we spent a lot of our time sightseeing. The accommodation was basic – Spartan I suppose – and in a private house. When I enquired why there was no light switch in the bedroom, the landlord smiled indulgently and explained that all I had to do was to move the wardrobe out from the wall, and I would find the switch behind it! The bathroom was down the hall and was shared by all and sundry, but then, what could one expect for the price?

So, the people were very friendly and the weather was warm, apart from the steady gale which blew for two hours *every* day! Of course that was siesta time, two to four, as we soon realized.

A visit to Knossos was mandatory and there was a regular bus service leaving from the town square, as it was then. On arrival at this bus station, we got tickets at a "hole in the wall" and wondering whether the service was national or private, I asked a native who spoke English how did one become a bus driver, "You buy a bus," he answered.

The bus was decorated inside with hand-knitted brightly coloured hangings and over the windscreen was a picture of the owner and the bus, the owner and his wife, a few religious pictures, a rosary beads and nearest to the driver, a calendar girl leaving nothing to the imagination.

The visit to Knossos was memorable, and the journey back took us two hours travelling through tiny mountain villages and terrifying roads with hairpin bends galore.

Later, we went to hire bicycles in order to visit the village of Kritsa, which we discovered was eight miles away – all uphill. The proprietor of the cycle hire place was a twelve year old with a red baseball cap and he quoted us fifteen shillings each for a day's rental. But then he took me aside and said:

"Sir, I have much better bikes which I keep hidden from the tourists and I would like you and your lady to have two of them – it's only an extra five shillings."

In the interest of safety, I agreed and arranged to pick

them up next morning. We did so next day and were about to depart when our friend said dramatically "Wait, Sir, you can go nowhere without your box of punctures." Having taken same on board, we cycled off and after doing the eight miles uphill, we arrived in an exhausted state in the village of Kritsa.

It was a quaint little village perched on the side of a mountain, and the centre, which held the only cafe and also the only tree, was a triangle where all the streets converged.

We saw people eating bread, salads, tempting omelets, tomatoes, and coffee, so we entered the triangle and I attempted to order from the man at the coffee counter. He nodded and said "Sit down please."

I returned to my seat and fifteen minutes later, when nothing had happened, I repeated my request, with the same result.

By now I was peckish and my fuse was quite short. But then we noticed a very old, very tiny woman tidying up tables, and my wife approached her and indicated what we wanted. She smiled and nodded and disappeared up the street.

We decided to give it five minutes more, and were about to leave when she arrived with two plates of exactly what we wanted. Then she brought the coffee, and the bread, and the bill and disappeared again.

Well, we had a handsome lunch and then I saw her again and I followed her out of curiosity. I discovered that the cafe was a family co-operative. Only the coffee came from the counter at the café, the omelets came from another house and the bread and salad came from yet another house – and the old lady was the key to it all.

The return journey downhill was pretty hairy and I was glad that we had those "extra good bikes" which had brakes! That evening, chatting to two other tourists, we found out that there was a bus to Kritsa three times a day, and the return fare was about two shillings!! We slept well that night!

We were not to know that on Crete this was Easter Week, two weeks later than ours and on the Saturday we understood there would be a Greek Orthodox Mass in the church on the hill. We considered that this would be better than no Mass, and we went there. We were not familiar with Greek Orthodox procedure, and were amazed to find the congregation standing and all chatting noisily and the altar was behind a screen. The priest came out every so often and there would be a kind of silence while he blessed the people. A choir of four men chanted incessantly during the service and at the end a casket like an Ark of the Covenant, covered with pink carnations, was carried out on the shoulders of six men. It was beautifully made of polished oak and was obviously very heavy. Four priests carrying lamps fell in behind and marched off downhill towards the centre of the village. It was almost dark at this time.

At the same time a second procession had started off from a church on the opposite hill and it was obvious they were going to meet at the centre. They did so and when they did, there was a cacophony of explosions as everyone fired explosive sparklers into the air. The assembled crowd then set off up towards the second church, where an outdoor altar was set up between two palm trees.

Having ascended to the altar the priests began a service while everyone chatted and fired more exploding sparklers, some of which I noticed had landed in one of the palm trees. Smoke began to rise and next thing, the whole tree began to blaze, but the priests continued undeterred. Then, up the hill came a group of men handling an antiquated fire pump, which was manually operated by six stalwarts. Out in front stood one guy pointing a hose up at the fire. The jet which came out of the hose formed an arc a full eight feet long, and merely drenched the approach to the altar. Consternation ensued and finally the fire died down and the "brigade" disappeared quietly though they did get a round of applause. The priests wound up the ceremony on schedule and the crowd dissolved amid great chat and laughter.

Many other things happened during those couple of weeks and all in all, we had a lovely time and it was a great holiday. I still have some of the souvenirs we bought.

Sangria

1976

Some years ago my wife and I were on holidays in Tenerife, and we stayed in a self-catering apartment, where we had breakfast, and it was our custom to dine out in the evenings. We enjoyed going to different restaurants each evening and sampling the local cuisine. I had a slight allergy to wine and so avoided it, but Sangria, well, that was a different matter. There was wine in it, sure enough, but it was tempered with dashes of Cointreau, Brandy, Vodka, Lemonade with lots of fresh fruit, crushed ice and whatever dribs and drabs the barman wanted to get rid of. I could drink it 'til the cows came home and I ordered it by the jug-full each evening. There was only one snag – it tended to give me nightmares!

One evening we were having a meal in a restaurant where the house recipe for Sangria was particularly nice. I was pouring myself a generous libation from the two litre jug when a complete stranger came up to our table,

"Do I hear an Irish voice?" he ventured.

"Yes, we're Irish," I replied

"My name is Monteith and I'm a dentist from Drogheda," he said, and I tried to keep a straight face and thought what a name for a dentist.

"I don't wish to intrude," he said, "but my wife and I haven't been here before, and we were wondering what is this drink you seem to be enjoying so much."

"It's Sangria," I said, "Here, try it" and I poured him a glass from which he sipped first, and then drained the glass, smacking his lips appreciatively.

"It's really beautiful," he said. "Could I have another wee drop to give my wife a taste?" I obliged and he carried it over to where his wife sat. We saw her drain the glass, which he then returned to our table.

"Well," he said, we never tried that before. We're not great drinkers, but Sangria will be our number one from

now on, and thank you very much for introducing us to it."

"Just one thing," I said, "too much of it can give you nightmares. In fact, I had a disturbing dream myself last night. I dreamt that my father, who is dead these years, came into my apartment for a chat and I told him to go back to wherever he came from as I was on my holidays."

"How extraordinary," said Monteith.

As we left, I smiled at the couple and said "Sweet Dreams." They laughed and wished us good night.

The next evening, although we had decided to try a new restaurant, we found ourselves entering the same one again. The pull of that Sangria was strong. And who should be there, complete with a large jug of Sangria, but Monteith. We paused to exchange pleasantries, when he said

"By the way, I've a message for you. My father said to tell your father he was asking for him! It's great stuff, I tell you!!

ISBN 1-905597-00-2

90000>

9 781905 597000